PRIMAL FORCE

ERIC S. BROWN

SEVERED PRESS
HOBART TASMANIA

PRIMAL FORCE

Copyright © 2021 Eric S. Brown

WWW.SEVEREDPRESS.COM

ISBN: 978-1-922551-84-9

PRIMAL FORCE

Private Walter Hickman's hair stood on end as he froze in his tracks. The night was dark and a hard rain fell. It had seeped through his clothes long before, drenching him and the others of his platoon to the bone. There seemed to be no end to the rain. It had been falling for the entire day and now continued on into the night. Walter hated it but right now. . . he had bigger worries to deal with. Sergeant Page had sent Harrison and himself on ahead of the rest of the platoon to make sure the path they were taking northward wasn't filled with booby traps. Their enemy in this war loved traps and were very creative at designing them. Punji sticks and grenades in a can were bad enough but they were nothing compared to the horror of the new mace traps being used in this region. A soldier could set off a tripwire and a huge ball covered in spikes would swing out of a tree. Its spikes would be driven into his body by the ball's weight, impaling the poor bastard where he stood, and then the ball would break open releasing a swarm of hornets to sting such an unlucky soldier and those around them even while he bled out. Walter hadn't seen a mace trap like that in person yet and hoped he never did but knew that there could one waiting on him even just a few steps ahead of him. It wasn't the thought of such a trap that had brought him to a stop though.

Glancing over at Harrison, Walter saw that his buddy looked just as spooked by the noise they had heard. There was a cave dangerously close to the path the rest of the platoon would soon be following behind them. They had both known they were going to have to check it out and make sure there wasn't a bunch of Viet Cong soldiers lurking inside of it, lying in wait for an ambush. No one had opened fire on them as they approached the cave's mouth. That had been a very good sign that it was clear but as they continued to creep closer to it, a low, guttural growl arose from somewhere within the cave. Walter had never heard anything like it before in his life. It was clearly some kind of animal that had made the noise but there was a disturbingly human edge to the growl. Walter didn't have clue what to do now. He couldn't see far enough into the shadows of the cave to see whatever had growled. Just opening up with an M-16 at whatever was in there was likely a very bad idea. They'd be telegraphing their position to any Viet Cong who were nearby and that was the last fragging thing Walter wanted to do. Even if the Viet Cong didn't show up and kill them, Sergeant Wright certainly would when the rest of their platoon came charging in to catch up with them and see what the hell was going on.

Harrison shrugged in the darkness letting Walter know the ball was in his court. Part of Walter wanted to back away from the cave and just keep moving. If the thing inside of it that growled was just an animal, odds were the beast wasn't dumb enough to attack a group of heavily armed humans as they came through. . . but the human-like edge to the growl kept Walter rooted where he was. The Viet Cong were tricky bastards. Walter motioned for Harrison to move on up and over to his position.

"What ya thinking, man?" Harrison whispered.

Walter frowned. "That we're going to have to either go in there or flush out whatever made that growl."

"I'm in favor of that second option," Harrison said.

"Yeah, but how?" Walter asked.

"Could just toss a grenade in there and see what happens," Harrison answered.

Walter shook his head. "Don't be an idiot."

"I'm not hearing a better plan," Harrison sighed.

Walter didn't answer. He just kept staring at the mouth of the cave. The low growl rose again from the deeper darkness beyond it.

"That thing is moving around in there," Harrison warned. "We may not have to. . ."

Before Harrison could finish his sentence, Walter caught a fleeting glimpse of glowing, yellow eyes as the thing in the cave charged them. The creature moved with such speed that neither of them managed to swing up their rifles in time to get a shot off at it. Walter threw his body to the left as the beast rammed into Harrison. It struck Harrison with such force that his body was lifted from the ground and flung backwards several yards through the air with the sharp cracking sound of breaking bones. Harrison splashed into the puddles that were scattered everywhere across the muddy jungle floor.

Walter spun about, bringing up the barrel of his rifle. His breath caught in his lungs and his eyes bugged as he got a look at the thing that had rammed into Harrison. The beast stood over six feet tall, yellow eyes burning in the night, and was covered head to toe in thick brown hair. Thick muscles bulged beneath the hair. The creature was like something out of a nightmare. It stood watching him, breathing heavily, waiting on him to make the next move as Harrison moaned in pain where he lay in the mud. As hurt as Harrison sounded, Walter was relieved to know that he was alive. The beast cocked its head, sniffing the air, still watching him closely as Walter stood as still as possible, not wanting to do anything that might launch the monster in front of him into another rampage. There were only a few feet between him and the beast as his mind raced to figure out if he could get enough shots into its body to stop the thing before it reached him if he tried. If the creature knew what his rifle was, there was no sign of it. The thing seemed utterly oblivious to the weapon aimed at it. Burt knew he had to do something other than just stand there staring at the monster until the thing finally decided to come at him. Time felt like it had slowed down as Walter opened fire. His first shot slammed into the monster's chest, splattering blood into the air. The beast staggered backwards but recovered impossibly fast, dodging the rest of the bullets Walter had sent its way by ducking and throwing itself out of their path. Walter stumbled, trying to put some distance between himself and the snarling beast as it sprang towards him. One of its hair-covered hands snatched the barrel of his M-16. Metal creaked as the beast bent the barrel upwards before wrenching the rifle from Walter's hand. The beast took a swing at him with its other hand, sharp claws gleaming in the dim, weak light of the moon that managed to seep through rain clouds above. Water splashed beneath his boots as Walter leaped back, narrowly avoiding the beast's attack. The beast tossed Walter's rifle aside, rising up to its full height with a fierce roar. Walter looked up into the creature's glowing yellow eyes as he yanked the knife strapped to the side of his boot from its sheath.

Desperate to stay alive, Walter found courage he didn't even know that he had, lunging forward to meet the beast as it came at him again. The blade of his knife sunk into the beast's side. Walter felt it scrape against bone as it slid between two ribs. A pained grunt escaped the beast. Walter screamed as claws clutched his arms and punctured

6

his skin. The beast was so strong that it broke both of his arms once, snapping them like twigs and bending them downward. Walter collapsed into the mud in front of the beast. The beast towered over him, breathing hard, the hilt of his knife still protruding from its side. Even through his own pain, Walter could see that the beast was hurting. The bullet it had taken and the blade buried in its side had taken their toll upon it. Walter couldn't get up. Hell, he couldn't even roll over. With both his arms so suddenly broken, it was taking all he had left just to stay conscious. Walter shrieked in pure terror as the beast dropped onto him, its claws tearing at his flesh, before its teeth closed on his throat.

****

Lieutenant Wagner trudged along through the jungle with the men under his command. Sergeant Page was on point with the rest of the small platoon spread out in a loose defensive formation. Wagner sighed heavily as he looked up at the sky. The rain just kept falling and he was sick to hell of it. He hadn't believed the stories of how bad it was out here until it was too late. Wagner had wanted to see action, be a hero, prove to himself that he was a real soldier. The bulk of his career in the Army had been spent pushing papers behind a desk. He'd called in a lot of favors to get command of this patrol. People he trusted had said he was crazy but Wagner hadn't listened to them. His mind had been filled with images of glory not rot growing in his boots and bugs swarming around him, wanting a taste of his blood, day after day. Only three days had passed since his patrol had left FireBase Tango but those days had felt like a month each. So far, they had run into the Viet Cong twice. Both were brief skirmishes without heavy losses. Wagner credited that fact to Sergeant Page. The guy was on his second tour and fragging well knew what he was doing. Wagner was more than happy to let Page handle keeping the men in line out here. He heard stories of commanding officers being shot in the back if their platoons thought they were incompetent and putting them in danger. Wagner didn't think he was doing that but guys who did this kind of crap all the time couldn't be expected to trust someone like him straight off without some proof that he knew was he was doing.

The sound of gunfire in the distance up ahead of the platoon's position caught everyone off guard.

Sergeant Page bellowed, "Hold your fire!"

It was obvious the gunfire was too far away to be a threat but that hadn't stopped a lot of soldiers from diving for cover anyway. Thankfully, no one was dumb enough to just start returning fire blindly.

Wagner rushed forward to join Sergeant Page at the head of the platoon's formation.

"What the hell was that?" Wagner asked.

"I'd say Walter and Harrison found themselves some trouble," Page grunted.

Wagner noticed that Page hadn't addressed him as sir but let it slide. He knew Page had his back out here and was fragging grateful for it.

"I only heard a few quick shots," Wagner commented.

"That's all there were," Page confirmed. "Reckon we'll have to see if that's a good thing or a very bad one."

"Those shots weren't that far away," Wagner said.

Page rose up from where he was crouching. "Everybody get moving, slow and easy."

Wagner agreed with Page's plan to creep up on whatever was up there ahead of them. There wasn't really another choice. If Walter and

Harrison were still alive, the two of them likely needed some back up right now. And they were his men. It was his job to haul their butts out of the fire.

The platoon moved slowly, everyone alert, eyes keeping close watch on the jungle around them. . .and not a fragging one of them was ready for what came next. Bates, one of the soldiers who had moved up to join him and Sergeant Page at the sharp end, died instantly. A rock flew out of the distant trees, smashing into his face. Bone crunched, folding inward from the force of the impact. Bates flopped over into the mud with half of the rock protruding from where his face had been and its other half buried deep in his skull.

More rocks came flying from out of the trees. One thudded into Lieutenant Wagner's shoulder. He grunted, wincing in pain, nearly knocked over by the impact.

"Take cover!" Sergeant Page shouted as he opened fire. His M-16 cracked in rapid succession as he poured lead into the trees ahead of the platoon's position. Another soldier cried out as a rock caught him in the chest with enough force to crack his ribs.

Wagner was trying to make sense of just what

in the hell was happening. The Viet Cong didn't attack with rocks! What was happening was utterly insane. He'd never heard of anything like it. All he could do was join Sergeant Page's attempt to drive away whoever was attacking them. His M-16 chattered as he emptied half of its magazine into the jungle, hoping to hit whatever was out there.

The attack stopped as suddenly as it had begun. The jungle fell quiet other than the moans of the wounded members of the platoon. . .and there was a lot of them. Over half of the twenty soldiers under Lieutenant Wagner's command had been hurt. Two of them had been killed outright. Wagner glanced over at where a private named Hanks lay, the side of his head dented inward, blood leaking out of his open mouth into the mud.

Lieutenant Wagner saw Sergeant Page look his way. The usually hard as nails NCO looked spooked. That worried Wagner more than anything. Page had seen a ton of crap out here in the jungle but apparently even he hadn't seen anything like what had just happened. Wagner started to call out to Page and order him to get the hell up from where he had taken cover and secure the area but things really went to hell.

The creatures dropped out of the trees right into the midst of the platoon, large, heavy feet splashing onto the muddy jungle floor. Wagner's eyes bugged in shock. There were a dozen of the monsters. Each of them stood between six and seven feet tall. They had overly long arms like those of an ape except that the fingers of their hands ended in gleaming, razor-like claws. Their bodies were covered head to toe in brown hair. In the darkness, the glow of their yellow eyes made Wagner wonder how he'd overlooked them in the trees until the monster had made their move but he knew the answer. His attention and that of the others had been focused on the threat of the Viet Cong they had expected not something as whacko and messed up as these. . .whatever the hell they were.

Sergeant Page rose to meet one of the monsters, putting several almost point blank shots into it. The monster squealed and flung itself away from him. Page wasn't about to let it get away though. He fired four more shots into its back. The monster thudded onto the ground, blood streaming out of its wounds. The man was a pro. Even facing literal monsters that had come out of nowhere, the sergeant managed to keep his crap together and get the job done. The sergeant impressed the hell out of Wagner.

One of the monsters roared, charging straight at him as Lieutenant Wagner's finger squeezed the trigger of his rifle. He fired three shots that all struck the beast, one tearing into its right shoulder, the other two thudding into its chest. They weren't enough to stop the monster or even really slow it down. Hairy hands grabbed hold of his M-16, yanking it from his grasp. The monster crushed the rifle where they closed upon it. Wagner gasped, staggering backwards, his right hand moving to yank his sidearm free of the holster on his hip. The Colt Commander lacked the power that his rifle had. Wagner didn't have high hopes that the pistol could stop the creature he was up against before the thing tore him apart limb by limb. Still, it was all he had and Wagner wasn't going to go down without a fight.

Sergeant Page took a quick look around. The monsters were murdering the other soldiers of the platoon with ease. He saw a soldier lifted up from the ground by one of the monsters to be ripped in half by its sheer brute strength. The soldier's entrails exploded out from beneath the tearing flesh of his abdomen, his shrieking wail of terror cut short by instant death. Another soldier died when large hands closed on the sides of his skull and crushed it like an over ripe melon, gore splattering everywhere.

Sergeant Page took aim at the monster which had torn the first soldier in half. He fired, putting a round in the thing's left eye, pulping it inside its socket. The monster stumbled, shaking its head in pain and rage, but didn't fall. Its head whipped around in his direction, one yellow eye still burning in the darkness. Sergeant Page held his ground as the creature rushed him. His M-16 barked in rapid succession. Bullets ripped at the monster's body, burying themselves in its gut and upper thighs. Sergeant Page had intentionally aimed low with his shots hoping to stop the monster before it reached him. The tactic paid off as the monster's legs gave out from under it. The monster's massive form smashed face down into the mud. Sergeant Page didn't give the creature a chance to recover and get up. He ran to where the beast lay, pressing the barrel of his rifle directly against its head and squeezed the weapon's trigger twice more. The bone of the monster's skull gave way as the two bullets blew through it, sending bits of shattered bone, blood, and brain matter spraying outward with them. The monster slumped fully back into the mud, its body lying there twitching in its death throes.

Someone screamed behind Sergeant Page. He whirled about to see Private Fisher die. A thick, hair-covered arm had been thrust through the center of his body. The monster that killed him yanked its blood slicked arm out of the young private's corpse, the gaze of its yellow eyes turning in his direction. Sergeant Page emptied what remained of his M-16's magazine into the thing. The monster slumped to its knees, blood pouring from the holes Sergeant Page had blown in its chest and guts. A low whine escaped its black lips. Whipping his sidearm out of its holster, Page fired three more shots into the monster's face, finishing it.

Lieutenant Wagner continued to backpedal as the monster he was facing closed on him. He had wounded the beast. That was for sure. Its movements were slower than they had been. The monster's right arm hung limply at its side from where a round from his M-16 had ripped into the muscles of its shoulder. If anything though, the creature seemed more intent than ever on making sure he died a painful death. Wagner held his Colt

Commander pointed at the monster in a trembling hand. Sergeant Page might be holding it together and kicking arse but he wasn't. The monsters were pushing the limits of what his mind could handle without snapping. Things like them had no right to exist in the real world. The monster snarled, showing him its razored teeth and lunged forward. Wagner met it with a series of shots from his pistol that pulped the thing's nose and slashed deep grooves of torn flesh across its cheeks. His aim had faltered after the first shot and he was about to pay the price for it. The monster reached Wagner, lashing out at him with the claws of its left hand. They entered his skin just below his shoulder and ripped downward across his chest. The swing was too fast to have even tried to dodge and just as quickly, the beast grabbed him. The monster's claws sunk into the soft flesh of Wagner's throat. He tried to suck in air but couldn't. The monster was choking him as it lifted him upwards. Wagner smashed a balled-up fist into the creature's wounded right shoulder. The beast lost its grip on him. Wagner toppled onto the ground at the monster's feet, clutching the side of his throat in an attempt to stop the blood flowing out of it.

Sergeant Page realized that he and Lieutenant

Wagner were the last two of the platoon left alive. Everyone else was dead, their bodies sprawled about, some missing limbs and heads. The monsters had taken losses of their own. He counted six hair-covered, bloodied corpses among the dead and another of the monsters, towering over Lieutenant Wagner, appeared to be badly wounded. Sergeant Page wanted to rush to Wagner's aid but couldn't. The other five monsters blocked his path, surrounding him. There wasn't even an opening he could use to make a run for it into the jungle. Sergeant Page's eyes scanned the muddy jungle floor around him searching for a weapon better than the half empty pistol he clutched in a white knuckled grip. Among the corpses, he spotted a shotgun next to Private Freeman. The poor bastard had had his guts opened up and they spilled out of him like purple, red slicked snakes. His mouth was open, jaws locked tight in death and the remnant of a scream. Sergeant Page shoved his pistol back into the holster on his hip and snatched up the shotgun, working its pump. He heard the sound of a round entering its chamber and grinned. The monsters attacked as one, rushing at him from all sides. Sergeant Page had hoped they would hold back and come at him one at a time. Sadly, that wasn't how things went down. The shotgun thundered. The monster he shot died instantly as its head splattered into a mess of bloody pulp and bone fragments. Sergeant Page tried to chamber another round but the monsters were too close and too fast. One of the things grabbed his right arm, yanking it loose from his body at its shoulder joint. Another swiped at the upper thigh of his left leg with its claws. Blood flew as they shredded the meat of his body there. A third beast plowed into him like a runaway eighteen-wheeler, taking Sergeant Page to the ground beneath it. He struggled against the monster's weight, trying desperately to shove it off of him. The monster was far too strong though. A hair-covered hand took hold of his head and began to slam it over and over into the ground. Sergeant Page's vision blurred as he began to give in to the pain that was coursing throughout his body. The world spun before his eyes as the monster released its hold on his head. The last thing Sergeant Page saw was the tips of the monster's claws as they descended into his eye sockets. His body lurched and bucked against the monster as it drove its fingers into his brain.

Lieutenant Wagner sat, one hand clamped to

the side of his throat, the other feeling around the ground for the pistol he had lost when the monster had attacked him. The monster had staggered away after he'd rammed a fist into its wounded shoulder. It spun back towards him now, yellow, feral eyes glowing with rage. His hand found the butt of the pistol. Lieutenant Wagner swung it up to meet the monster as it leaped at him. The pistol cracked once and then clicked empty. That single shot though was enough. It caught the beast in the underside of its chin, exiting the backside of its skull right at the base of its neck. Lieutenant Wagner heaved himself to the left as the monster's heavy corpse slammed into the ground where he had been. He scrambled to his feet, one hand still clutching his throat. On some level, Wagner knew he was already dead. Bright red blood seeped through the fingers of the hand pressed to his neck. For all his effort, the pressure he was applying hadn't done crap in stopping its flow. Even so, he ran for his life, stumbling away into the jungle. He hoped the other monsters were too occupied by eating what was left of Sergeant Page to notice. And they were eating the sergeant. Wagner had caught a glimpse of a monster holding on to one of the sergeant's arms, gnawing the meat off of it.

Not daring to look back, Lieutenant Wagner kept moving. His legs felt like jelly and each step he took made the world before his eyes spin about him faster. He never saw the rock that came flying through the trees from behind him before it cracked open his skull in an explosion of blood and gore.

****

Major Devin Callen stood at attention in front of Colonel Evans' desk inside the Tactical Command Center of Firebase Maria. Callen didn't care for being so unexpectedly and hurriedly summoned to the T.O.C. like he had been. Sadly, there was nothing he could do or say about it. He and his men were supposed to be getting ready to ship out for a much needed five days of R&R at China Beach. They'd earned it too but that didn't mean crap if the colonel needed them.

"At ease," Colonel Evans sighed.

"You sent for me, sir," Major Callen said.

"I did," Colonel Evans smiled. "Take a seat, Major. We've got a lot to talk about."

Major Callen plopped into the chair he had been standing next to. He stared across the desk, waiting on the colonel to deem it time to tell him what the hell was going on.

"Lieutenant Wagner took a platoon out on patrol a few days ago," Colonel Evans said.

"I'd heard about that. He was some kind of paper pusher, right? Had to pull some strings to get the command." Callen produced a cigarette from the pocket of the vest he wore and lit up, sucking a deep drag from it. "Let me guess, he and his platoon got lost out there?"

"Yeah," Colonel Evans nodded. "But that's not why you're here."

Major Callen raised an eyebrow.

"You're here because his isn't the only patrol we've lost in the last few days." Colonel Evans reached to roll out a map over the top of his deck and stabbed at section of jungle on it. "We've lost three patrols, including that fragging desk jockey's, in this area."

"Three?" Major Callen asked.

"Three," Colonel Evans confirmed. "I think there's something going on in that area that needs to be dealt with or at least smoked out so that we can see what it is. Could be the Viet Cong are building up their forces there, getting ready for a big time offensive against us. Could just be some really crappy luck on our part with those patrols. But we need to know for sure about whatever is happening in that region. And that's where you come in, Major."

"Sir, with all due respect, my men are beat. They're up for some R&R and all of them really need it," Major Callen protested as politely as he could.

"I am aware of that, Major," Colonel Evans scowled. "Frankly though, you're the best I've got available to send. The copters we've got here can drop you just outside the region where the other platoon went missing. I need you to go in, find out what the deal is, and get the hell out. I'll have the copters standing by for pickup, my word on that."

"Doesn't sound like I have much of a choice, sir," Major Callen frowned.

Colonel Evans laughed. "You don't. I want you and your men ready to be aboard those copters by nightfall. You'll be heading out tonight."

"Understood, sir," Major Callen acknowledged the colonel's orders.

Major Callen left the Tactical Command Center feeling defeated but more than anything, he was worried. Patrols vanished. That happened in war. . . but three of them in as many days. . .that meant something was surely going on in the area where they'd been lost. He didn't relish the thought of not knowing just what the hell he was about to lead his men into. Unknowns got you killed in war. That was just a simple fact.

Firebase Maria was a huge place. It was one of the more permanent bases that had been established in this region. Despite its size or perhaps because of it, the firebase was set up in the standard star formation with a centralized Howitzer to fire illumination rounds and the rest fanning outward at the edges of the large base around it. The base's personnel numbered close to six hundred by the time you factored in all the support, brass, and pilots. It didn't have just a couple of landing pads like most firebases. The firebase had its own squadron on site in addition to the ones constantly coming and going from it. Six UH-1 Huey copters and two Cobra gunships sat ready any time Colonel Evans needed them.

The firebase's buildings were spread out behind earthen barriers and barbed wire. Callen had heard of attacks on other firebases but the Viet Cong would have to be fools to make a move against Maria. Vietnam was a war of fronts everywhere but even so, Firebase Maria was at least currently some distance from areas where there was known to be Viet Cong activity.

Everyone on the base felt safe. As Major Callen walked across the base to the bunker where he'd left his men, there were soldiers being drilled, marching along and singing, others sitting about drinking and playing cards; heck, there was even a few scattered shirtless troops sunbathing.

Major Callen approached the door to the bunker where his men were holed up, resting. Outside it stood Sergeant Giffen and Corporal Dixon. The two of them always struck him as an odd pair though they were as close as brothers. Sergeant Giffen was a short, burly man with thick, muscled arms. Corporal Dixon on the other hand was as long legged as a giraffe. Dixon was as fast as Giffen was strong. Their combat styles were just as different as their appearances. Dixon took the laid back, easy going approach while Giffen didn't take any crap . . . at all. Everyone in the platoon knew if the quiet, almost always angry little man spoke, you'd dang well better be listening and do what he said. Giffen and Dixon saw him walking up to the bunker. Dixon flashed him a wry grin and waved like a schoolkid. Callen ignored him.

"That look on your face says it all," Giffen rumbled. "When are we rolling out?"

Callen snorted. "We're not rolling at all, Giffen. We're getting a lift from the Air Cav."

"Far out," Dixon's grin grew wider.

The corporal loved flying. He seemed more at home on a helicopter than anywhere else in the world. He'd put in for a transfer numerous times since coming under Callen's command. Callen didn't take it personally but had still denied them all. Dixon was just too fragging good of a scout to give up to the Air Cav or anyone else. Callen needed him right where he was. Besides, without Dixon around, Giffen would be unbearable. The long-legged joker was the counterbalance to the little man's grimness.

Giffen cut his eyes at Dixon. "Do you have to sound so happy about our arses being sent back into the bush so soon?"

"You gotta lighten up, man," Dixon laughed. "And learn to make the most of what life throws at you."

"Frag you," Giffen muttered.

"So what's the gig?" Dixon asked.

"Some Shake and Bake type lieutenant took a platoon out, never came back," Major Callen answered.

"Typical," Dixon shook his head. "And now

we're on search and rescue, eh?"

"Not exactly," Callen frowned. "His platoon isn't the only one that's gone missing in the area he was sent to. Two others vanished without a trace there too. . .all in a matter of days. Colonel Evans suspects that good old Chuck has something big cooking in that area. Wants us to recon the place, find out what Chuck's up to before it bites us."

"Cool," Dixon nodded. "That makes sense."

"Why us?" Giffen grunted.

"Why do you think?" Callen threw back at him.

Giffen sighed. "Sometimes it truly sucks to be the best, sir."

"Aye," Callen smiled. "That is does. Go get the boys up and let them know the score. We'll be flying out as soon as it gets dark."

Fox came sauntering out of the bunker with a beer in his hand. He was smiling like tomorrow was Christmas morning and he was a five-year-old, rich kid. Handsome was an understatement where Fox was concerned. Bright blue eyes beneath a mop head of blonde hair, tan skin, and enough suave to woo the most frigid Donut Dolly in Nam out of her clothes. Fox wasn't much of a fighter but he was as brave as they came and a medic of the highest caliber. Callan has seen Fox pull off miracles he wouldn't have believed possible.

"Hey, Major!" Fox beamed. "You come to join the party?"

Looking around, Fox saw the expressions on the other men's faces.

"Ah crap," Fox shook his head sadly.

"Fox, where did ya go, man?" Sheen asked, stumbling out of the bunker after Fox. He was so drunk that Sheen looked hardly able to stay on his feet.

"Party's over, boys," Giffen snapped, moving to snatch the can of beer Sheen was barely holding onto out of his hand. "Fox, get this A-hole sobered up A.S.A.P."

"Yes sir," Fox nodded, turning to lead Sheen back inside the bunker.

****

Callen's platoon was understrength. . . way understrength by the usual standards. It consisted of only eighteen men including himself, Sergeant Giffen, and Corporal Dixon. They'd picked up two newbies here at Firebase Maria. That brought them back to twenty men, but he wasn't ready to fully count the two newbies yet. He'd read their files in great detail. Major Callen, unlike many officers in Nam, liked to know everything he could about the men under him from the get go and actually made it a point to do so. The first of the newbies went by the nickname Lovecraft. He reminded Callen of an educated version of Corporal Dixon. Lovecraft had gotten his name from that of his favorite author. The kid was supposedly constantly reading pulp horror. He'd made a joke once about worrying that his previous platoon would run into something called shoggoth in the jungle and his nickname was born. Lovecraft wore thick rimmed glasses and was the platoon's radio man. Callen had no issue with Lovecraft. Geeky weirdos were something that you came across no matter where you were. The other newbie though, Allen, was the sort that a good C.O. never wanted in their unit. Allen was one of the ugliest bastards Callen had ever seen. The features of his face were sharp and long. Allen was thin and didn't look to be much of a fighter but there was a feralness about him that spoke volumes about just how dangerous he was. The guy was creepy as hell too. There was something off about him, more than just an addiction to combat like some guys got out here.

According to his file, in an after-action report by his former C.O., a Lieutenant named Mintz, the last firebase Allen had been at had come under attack. Allen had been a no show on the line defending the place. Everyone had thought he had lost it and bugged out. What had actually happened though was half a dozen Viet Cong who had managed to get into the firebase had come at him in the bunker where Allen was sleeping. The creep had taken all six of them out. Lieutenant Mintz had found Allen in the bunker, surrounded by their cut up and mutilated corpses, just sitting there, cleaning his knife with a big ole smile on his face. Mintz had recommended, quietly of course, a Section Eight for Allen after seeing that. Allen hadn't been given one though. The Brass had just transferred him out of Lieutenant Mintz's command and now Callen was stuck with him. Callen had asked Giffen for his gut take on Allen and whether or not he was psycho as Mintz's report made him out to be. Giffen had shrugged and just told him that it took killers to win a war. That was enough for Callen to feel at least somewhat better about the newbie. Giffen was a good judge of things like that and he clearly didn't think Allen was something that they couldn't make use of.

As the sun sank beneath the distant hills, Major Callen stood watching his men board the copters they'd be riding out. They were separating up into three squads, each one aboard a different Huey. A Cobra gunship would be flying with them as an escort. That fact alone showed just how much Colonel Evans wanted the intel that they were being sent out to get. If the Viet Cong were up to something as big as what the colonel feared. . .Major Callen frowned and decided he didn't want to think about that. Things were going bad enough in Nam already. Sergeant Giffen was leading Alpha Squad while Corporal Dixon had Gamma. He, himself, was riding with Beta Squad. No one but him liked the names Callen had given the squads but, well, they could go screw themselves. It was his call after all. Rank had its privileges.

Lovecraft was part of Beta Squad. As the platoon's radio operator, he had to be. Callen needed the newbie close. The rest of Beta Squad was composed of the Henry brothers, Burt, and Stu. It was the smallest of three squads as both Alpha and Gamma numbered seven soldiers, not six. Callen followed the others of Beta Squad onto their copter, taking a seat next to Lovecraft. The Henry brothers were cutting up and talking smack, elbowing each other and cursing to the point where the bird's door gunner looked like he wanted to figure out a way to turn his outward facing M-60 around on them. Burt sat silently, inspecting his M21. He was very much in love with the rifle. Anyone could see it from how he touched the weapon while cleaning it. Burt always had it loaded with a twenty round magazine instead of the smaller ones that many snipers used. Callen had to admit, the M21 was a beautiful weapon but he'd be sticking with his M-16. If he were honest with himself, Callen envied Burt. The rifleman was the best shot he'd ever seen both in and out of the service. Burt was a pro too, focused on his "work" as he liked to call it. Now, Stu. . .well, Stu was Stu. The Texan wore a cowboy style hat which he had pulled down over his eyes, slumping in his seat, grabbing some sleep. He, too, carried his own personal weapon instead of a standard issue one like Burt. The Texan's rifle of choice was a Winchester 30-30. It fit him well.

Major Callen strapped in as the helicopter's blades began to whirl. He glanced over at Lovecraft as the radio operator pushed his glasses into a higher position on his nose with the middle finger of his left hand.

The UH-1 Huey lifted off from the firebase's landing pad. The Cobra gunship escorting the group of Hueys was already in the air, leading the way. Major Callen leaned over closer to Lovecraft.

The geeky radio operator met his eyes.

"Heard a lot about your skill with a radio," Major Callen commented. "You're supposed to be one of the best in Nam."

"Thank you, sir," Lovecraft beamed. "I was studying to be an engineer back home before. . ."

Callen made the wrong assumption. "You got drafted."

"No, sir," Lovecraft shook his head. "Before I signed up."

Eyes going wide, Callen stared at Lovecraft in shock. "You volunteered for this crap? Why in the devil would you do that with the kind of skills you've got?"

"Wanted to learn how to fight, sir," Lovecraft shrugged. "I was tired of getting bullied and pushed around."

"And have you?" Callen asked.

Lovecraft shrugged again but didn't give him a real answer.

"How about you, sir?" Lovecraft changed the subject. "Were you drafted? Is that why you're here?"

Callen grunted. "No, I wasn't. My old man was one hell of a bastard. I needed out and had nowhere else to run to."

"I'm sorry, sir," Lovecraft said sincerely. "I can imagine what that must have been like."

"I very much doubt that, Lovecraft," Callen frowned. "Doesn't matter though. We both made our choices and now have to do our best to honor that."

Lovecraft nodded and then said, "Mind if I inquire as to where we're headed? I heard some, uh. . . rather concerning rumors."

Major Callen flashed a grin. "I'm sure you heard several platoons have vanished, all close together and in a small amount of time. We're going to find out why and what happened to them."

Lovecraft gestured at Burt and Stu. "Are they always like this? I mean I've seen troops who are used to the war but those guys. . . Burt looks like he's praying to his rifle and that guy from Texas is just taking a nap."

Laughing loudly, Callen punched Lovecraft's shoulder. "They aren't worried because this is all second nature to them now. They're the best and they know it. It's the Viet Cong that should be shaking in their boots."

The flight took a couple of hours. The group of copters flew high above the dense jungle below. As they arrived at their destination, the Cobra gunship took up a defensive position, hovering, pivoting around in the sky, covering the trees around the clearing where the others' birds touched down one after another. Xenon searchlights lit up the area where the birds were making their drops. Alpha Squad's Huey landed first, dispatching Sergeant Giffen and his men. They rushed out of the copter to secure the landing zone. Major Callen's copter came in for a landing as the one that had deposited Alpha Squad flew away. The Henry brothers were the first off of it with Burt following closely on their heels. Stu was the last one off their copter behind Major Callen and Lovecraft. All of them hurried to clear the LZ for the final Huey bringing in Corporal Dixon and Gamma Squad.

Sergeant Giffen came running up to Major Callen. "The area is as secure as it can be, sir. No sign of the Viet Cong."

"Good," Major Callen said and turned to

Lovecraft. "I need you to get on the horn. Let the colonel know we've arrived and are heading in."

"Yes sir!" Lovecraft snapped.

Callen stood for a moment watching the copters disappear into the night sky above as they hightailed it back towards Firebase Maria. They were alone now, arses hanging in the wind. It was on them and no one else to get the job done.

"Let's move!" Callen barked, swinging a hand around above his head, gesturing for the squads to form up and march into the cover of the jungle. In the clearing of the landing zone, they were little more than sitting ducks if there were some Viet Cong troops hiding in the trees. Of course, an ambush wasn't the only threat in the darkness of the jungle. There could be all manner of traps just waiting to be stumbled into. Sergeant Giffen took point, he and Alpha Squad leading the rest. Major Callen was glad to have the sergeant out front. The burly, little man fragging well had a keen eye for booby traps. And odds were, Sheen was right at his side. Sheen might be a drunk and weedhead but in the field he could be a valuable asset to the point it had kept him from being booted out of the platoon. Sheen had grown up in the South in a family of bear hunters. When he was sober, Sheen

35

was a great tracker and that made him great as trap spotter too.

Lovecraft hurried up to Callen. "Sir!" the radio operator called to get his attention.

Major Callen turned his head to glance at Lovecraft.

"The colonel has been informed that we've arrived, sir," Lovecraft reported.

Callen nodded. "Stick with me. kid. I mean it. That radio of yours is the only lifeline we've got if things go badly."

"Yes sir," Lovecraft snapped, falling in at his side.

The platoon's destination was at least a few hours march to the north. The copters had dropped them as close as they could but they still had a ways to go. The night was muggy and humid. The moon was bright in the sky above but Major Callen could feel the rain that would soon be moving in, in his bones. It was all the more reason to keep hauling butt as quickly as they reasonably could without too much risk.

The Henry brothers were keeping their mouths shut and weren't up to their normal bickering. Larry, the older brother, was packing an M-60 at the ready. The Pig, as it was nicknamed, was heavy to carry but Larry was a big guy and used to its weight. You could tell that by simply watching how he held the weapon. Harry, the younger of the two, had a Thumper in his hands. The M-79 grenade launcher looked like a sawed-off shotgun but was effective at a range of up to three hundred and fifty meters. It was a difficult weapon to reload but amazing at clearing areas of dead space where the enemy could be lying low in tall grass. Harry's only other weapons were a pair of pistols holstered on his belt and a large knife sheathed on the side of his right boot.

Major Callen looked over his shoulder and saw Corporal Dixon approaching him. There was a look of concern on Dixon's face. Callen slowed his pace just enough to let Dixon catch up.

"Something wrong, Corporal?" Callen asked.

"I've got a bad feeling about this one, sir," Dixon told him. "Something ain't right out here."

Callen frowned. Had it been someone else, he would have dismissed such a warning out of hand. Coming from Dixon though. . . it was worrisome. He had known the corporal a long time and knew that Dixon didn't spook easily or without reason.

"Not much we can do about that, Corporal," Callen said. "Just stay sharp and keep your head down."

Dixon nodded, falling back.

"Sir," Lovecraft whispered.

"What is it, Lovecraft? You got a bad feeling too?" Callen sighed.

"I was hoping I could ask you a personal question, sir," Lovecraft said.

Glad for a shift of mental gears, Callen answered, "Go ahead. Spit it out."

"One doesn't see too many people of your rank out here leading platoons on patrol. Isn't it sort of below you?" Lovecraft asked.

Major Callen chuckled. "The big brass knew they'd never really be able to get me out of the field short of sending me home. . . so I guess you could say they decided to make use of me. I got to handpick the bulk of my platoon and now we run the ops that are too important to be left to just anyone."

"You really like it out here, putting your life on the line?" Lovecraft was looking at him as if he were insane.

Callen didn't answer. He didn't have a clue how to. How could you express to someone feelings as deep as the one that drove him? Even if he did, would someone like Lovecraft understand?

The truth wasn't anything so simple as serving his country, taking care of his men, or any other clich1200985112 é.

Lovecraft continued to stare at him as if expecting more of an answer. Callen didn't oblige him.

Before Lovecraft could say anything more, a call came in over the radio that the newbie was carrying.

"Beta on the ground, this is Death Machine in the sky. Come in, over?" a voice called out through a slight crackle of static.

Death Machine was the call name of the Cobra gunship that had been their escort during the flight in. If the copter was attempting to contact them, it sure as hell wasn't for anything good. It went against the norm. They hadn't been ordered to keep radio silence but Callen assumed such an order had certainly been implied.

Lovecraft handed him the radio.

"This is Major Callen," he said. "What's the deal, Death Machine?"

"We're passing over some whacked out movement down there to your west. Never seen anything like it. The fragging trees are shaking," Death Machine's pilot answered. "No clear visual on the cause. Pretty sure it's not Charlie but wanted to give you a head's up."

"Copy that, Death Machine," Callen responded, "And thanks. Beta out."

"What the hell was that about?" Corporal Dixon asked, having overhead what the gunship's pilot had told him.

Callen shrugged. "No fragging idea. Whatever they saw from up there must have scared the hell out of them."

"No kidding," Dixon frowned. "That's some messed up . . ."

Not waiting for Dixon to finish, Callen hurried towards the front of the platoon to where Sergeant Giffen was. Giffen, eyes sharp, saw him coming and gave the position for the platoon to hold up where it was.

Callen was about to give Giffen the sitrep and bring him up to speed when he heard what the Cobra's pilot had warned him about. In the distance, screeches and howls rang out in the night. For a split second, the sound was so loud it seemed the ground beneath their feet was shaking. Then it all fell silent as suddenly as it had begun.

Giffen and Callen exchanged an equally concerned and confused look.

"What the. . .?" Giffen whispered.

Callen held up a finger, telling him to shut up.

Both of them listened intently to the night. There was a faint rustling that still seemed to be a decent distance away. The noise was clearly the sound of a large group of *somethings* moving and fast too. It grew more distant, fading away to silence once more. Callen and Giffen kept quiet for another full minute, listening for the noise to start up again. . . but it didn't. Whatever had made it was gone now, too far away to be heard.

Callen looked around at his men. Even Sergeant Giffen seemed freaked out by what had just happened. They were all looking to him for an answer as to what it was and what they should do. Callen didn't have those answers to give. He didn't have a clue what had been out there in the darkness, rushing through the jungle. Callen was pretty sure though that whatever it was hadn't been human. Human beings didn't make noise like that.

"Sir?" Lovecraft stammered, walking up to him.

Waving the radio operator's question aside, Callen barked, "Everybody get your crap together. We need to keep moving. Eyes and ears sharp, people."

Sergeant Giffen got the platoon back underway before returning to taking point. Callen and Lovecraft held back to make sure they were in the center of its formation. Honestly, Callen would rather have been on point with the Sergeant. If there was something crazy out there in the jungle to be dealt with, it was his job to make sure they could handle it.

****

As dawn broke over the jungle, Sergeant Giffen brought the platoon to a halt. The rain everyone had been expecting had held off. Gray clouds were thick in the sky above but rays of sunlight were beginning to pierce through giving hope that the day wasn't going to entirely suck.

"We gotta be getting close," Corporal Dixon said.

Sergeant Giffen nodded. "Yep. That desk jockey's platoon had to have gotten lost near here."

"The others too," Major Callen sighed.

"Haven't seen any real sign of Chuck out here yet," Dixon pointed out.

That worried Callen. The area had indeed been much clearer of any kind of Viet Cong presence than he had expected. They hadn't even run into traps and that was odd enough alone to be a perplexing sign.

"This whole thing is fragged," Sergeant Giffen snorted.

Callen couldn't argue with the sergeant. Nothing was playing out as he had expected it to. Still, having pushed through the night, it was time to let the men get some rest, no matter how little that might be. Callen didn't care for being out in the open as much as they were but there was nothing for that.

"Fragged or not, we've got a job to do," Callen said. "Dixon?"

"Figured we would be here for a few hours, sir," Dixon told him. "I sent out two man teams to the north and the west."

"Good," Callen nodded. "The more we know about this area the better. Maybe we'll get lucky and they'll stumble onto somewhere we can truly hole up in for a bit. In the meantime. . ."

"In the meantime, sir," Sergeant Giffen said forcefully, "you're going to get some rest."

"Sergeant, . . ." Callen started to argue but decided against it. He was exhausted and who knew when any of them might get the chance to catch some Zs again. Finally, Callen responded,

"Fine. I'll find a comfortable spot and get settled in, Sergeant. Find me and wake me up the second those scout teams come back. That's an order."

"Yes sir," Sergeant Giffen beamed, happy to have gotten him to agree to get some rest.

Callen watched Giffen and Dixon go to make sure the makeshift camp was as secure as it could be then turned his attention to finding somewhere to settle in. He found a comfortable looking spot on the jungle floor and got out his bedroll. Callen spread it out and laid down on it. The sun had continued to break through the gray clouds. Forcing himself to close his eyes, Callen tried to get some sleep. His exhausted state helped. He was out in no time. Unfortunately, his sleep wasn't really restful. In his dreams, he relived the platoon's run in with whatever the hell it had run into last night. He could hear the animal-like shrieks and howls among the trees all around him, the mad rustling of things dashing by. Whether it was a creation of his own mind or a subconscious memory from the night before, Callen could see glowing, yellow eyes in the trees. The sight of them scared the utter living hell out of him. Callen shivered where he lay, rolling about on his bedroll. A low, terrified moan escaped his lips. His dream self stood exactly where he had in the jungle when the encounter had actually happened, only now, Callen could see into the depths of the trees. Through them, he caught glimpses of things that chilled him to the bone, things not human, things that shouldn't exist in the real world.

"No!" Callen shouted, jerking away, and nearly springing all the way onto his feet.

"Major!" Lovecraft cautioned him, moving to shove him back onto the ground.

Callen stared up into the geeky radio operator's eyes, not knowing what was real and what wasn't.

"Are you okay, sir?" Lovecraft asked, his hands clutching Callen's shoulders.

Sweat flew from Callen's hair as he shook his head to clear it before growling, "Get your hands off of me, Lovecraft."

Eyes going wide, Lovecraft released him and backed off. The kid looked immensely worried about him.

"Are you alright?" the young geek pressed him. "The sergeant and corporal aren't here right now. Should I go get them?"

"I'm fine," Callen rasped. "Just a bad dream."

"You sure, sir?" Lovecraft asked.

"Kid, one day, if you live through all the crap I

have, you'll have nightmares too," Callen assured the young radio operator. That was true too except that the nightmare he'd just had weighed on him heavily. There was something about it that was as messed up as the insane encounter with whatever the hell passed them by in the jungle last night. Callen wanted to ask Lovecraft if he'd seen anything when it happened but he didn't. No one had come forward with admissions of seeing things like Callen saw in his dreams but that didn't mean they hadn't. Out here, if somebody started talking about monsters, it usually meant that they'd lost it and were likely about to be the next person to die.

"I understand that, Major," Lovecraft said quietly. "It's just. . ."

"Just what?" Callen snapped.

"That didn't look like just any nightmare," Lovecraft told him.

"Forget about it," Callen ordered the young radio operator.

"Yes sir," Lovecraft nodded.

Callen considered trying to go back to sleep but that seemed impossible to him now. He wiped the sweat from his face and shook out his hair again.

****

Burt and Allen moved through the jungle. Their movements were as close to being completely silent as human beings were capable of. Both of them were fragging good at their jobs. They had never worked alone together before but each could sense that the other was a professional. Burt was the platoon's sniper and primary scout while Allen was simply a killer.

The sun had risen high in the sky, finally breaking completely through the clouds. The air was humid and muggy. They'd been sent out to get an idea of what lay in this area. The major was likely hoping that they would find an abandoned village or building of some kind where the platoon could securely hole up and use as a basecamp. Of course, they were searching for signs of the missing platoons as well. That was why their platoon had been sent out here.

They were covering a large amount of ground for two guys on foot so far. Burt was ahead of Allen by several yards. He was the first to notice the stench in the air. His nose wrinkled as it hit him. He held up a hand, signaling for Allen to hold back. The sniper wanted to check things out for himself. There was no need for both of them to go wading into trouble. Greatly slowing his pace, Burt kept moving forward. There was something lying on the jungle floor. Burt slid behind the trunk of the closest tree, taking cover as he realized it was a body. The crumpled, mangled thing had once been a man. He wore a blood smeared Viet Cong uniform. There were pieces of a shattered rifle scattered near where he lay. Burt stared at the corpse and broken rifle trying to piece together exactly what had happened in the small clearing. There was a slight rustle in the brush behind him. Burt glanced over his shoulder to see Allen moving up to join him. Neither of them spoke but they didn't need to. Burt nodded at the small clearing and Allen picked up on what was going on.

The two of them left their cover together, approaching the corpse. Burt reached it first, squatting down to examine the dead Viet Cong's body. Maggots crawled all over the corpse and insects swarmed about it. Burt waved what he could of the insects away as he began to look over the dead man's body. Something had smashed in the bones of the man's chest. . .from the look of it, with a single blow too. His right hand and lower arm were crushed. As disturbing as those things were, they were nothing compared to the man's face. Something that had to be huge, looked to have literally taken a bite out of it. The man's nose was gone leaving only teeth marks and a hole of torn flesh where it had been. Burt had seen a lot of things in the war that had hardened him but this. . .he swallowed hard as bile rose inside his throat, forcing it back down.

Allen stood over him, eyes scanning the trees surrounding them, standing ready to deal with anything that might be lurking in them. Burt was glad that Allen was with him. He'd heard the stories the other guys in the platoon told about the newbie's lethalness. Getting back to his feet, Burt motioned for them to get moving again. His gut told him that if they headed on in this direction that they were going to find a lot more than just this one Viet Cong soldier. . . and it was right.

Burt and Allen emerged into a larger clearing where something akin to a slaughter appeared to have taken place. There were another seven corpses, all Viet Cong, strewn about the clearing. A quick look at them showed that they were even more torn up than the corpse the two of them had just left behind. Some of the dead Viet Cong were missing limbs. One was missing his head. All of them appeared have been gnawed upon by some kind of large animal. . . or maybe a pack of them. They'd put up a fight. There were spent casings in the grass. Whatever had hit them, it had come at them hard and fast. The poor bastards didn't look to have had a chance. Burt was all for killing the Viet Cong but not like this. No one deserved to die like these guys had. Allen gave a quiet grunt, getting Burt's attention. He pointed at a track in the mud near the body that Burt was looking over. Burt couldn't believe he had missed it. The gory mess of the Viet Cong distracting him was the only excuse his mind could come up with.

The track was much larger than any human foot could make. It was deeper too. Whatever had left it had some serious mass to it. Yet it looked roughly human-shaped. Burt knew there were apes in Nam. He'd never seen one but knew they were out there. There was a story of a firebase being attacked by the things, keeping outside of its perimeter, hurling rocks at the troopers defending it. Still, he had never heard of apes that *ate* people. And these poor, dead, Viet Cong bastards had been partially eaten after they were killed.

Allen placed a hand on his shoulder. Burt nearly jumped out of his skin but managed not to cry out despite being so startled. He looked up at Allen. The killer's expression was hard and worried. Allen gestured at the tree line. As he did, Burt sensed it too. They were being watched by something out there in the jungle around the clearing. Burt rose slowly to his feet from where he had been kneeling over the track in the mud. He tilted his head back in the direction they had come. Allen nodded. Together, they began a cautious, creeping retreat. Burt felt vulnerable as hell. He couldn't see a blasted thing in the trees but knew something was there. It sure wasn't the Viet Cong or they would have been fired upon already. That creeped out Burt even more than he already was because it almost surely meant the watchers were likely the animals that had ripped apart the Viet Cong soldiers in the clearing. There had been eight of them, all armed, not counting any others he and Allen hadn't found that might be hidden in the brush. He and Allen were alone out here. The rest of the platoon was too far away to even hear their gunshots much less come charging to their aid.

Something moved amid the trees across the clearing from them. Even with his keen eyes, Burt barely caught a glimpse of the creature. He could tell that whatever the thing was, it was big and had a roughly humanoid shape. Surprisingly, Allen had held his fire, not opening up on the creature. Burt wondered if he had underestimated the killer. Maybe there was more to him than the perverse love of death and killing that was his rep. Opening fire on the creature would have only pressed the beast into attacking them and given its cover, Allen likely wouldn't have hit it anyway. The creature had ducked further into the cover of the trees, out of their sight. Burt knew it was still there though.

Burt glanced over at Allen. The killer's expression was grim. He didn't seem to care for their current mess any more than Burt did himself. Unless they wanted to try to engage the creature, which didn't seem wise to Burt, their only choice was to continue the slow, backwards retreat they had begun. Neither one of them was expecting or prepared for what happened next. A rock came flying towards them. Allen jerked his head to the side, narrowly avoiding having his skull reduced to pulp and broken bone. His reflexes were sharper than any Burt had ever seen. Another rock followed the first as Allen cried out, "Run!"

The two of them spun about, changing their cautious retreat into an all out mad dash for the cover of the jungle behind them. Allen was several steps ahead of him as Burt ran, legs pumping beneath him. He saw Allen dive into the trees just as a rock slammed into his back. Its impact was cushioned by his backpack or the impact might have broken his spine. Even so, it knocked him from his feet and sent Burt sprawling, face first, onto the ground. He landed with a loud grunt as his breath left his lungs. Struggling to suck air back in, Burt rolled over, the barrel of his rifle swinging up, aimed at the other side of the clearing where the rock had come from. His weapon was a sniper rifle that lacked the fully automatic fire of Allen's M14. Burt's finger worked the trigger of his M21, firing a trio of shots at the distant trees. He heard bark splintering but no cries or shrieks. The best he could hope for was that he had given whatever was attacking them a reason to back off. Burt ceased firing, rolling over onto his stomach, crawling onward towards where Allen was. Allen had taken cover by the trunk of a larger tree, waiting on him to catch up. The killer was still holding his fire though which again surprised Burt and this time. . .sort of ticked him off. Had the guy not heard of cover fire?

Allen left his cover as Burt crawled close to

him. He yanked Burt to his feet and shoved him deeper into the cover of the trees. Burt had caught his breath and wasn't painfully sucking in gulps of air anymore but his back ached like hell. Even through the cushion of his backpack, the rock that hit him had done some damage. He was going to have a heck of a bruise, assuming of course that he lived through the next few minutes. The beast that had surely thrown the rock was shrieking somewhere in the jungle nearby. Burt didn't trust his judgement on which direction the cries were coming from. It seemed like the cries were coming from every direction at once.

"Sounds like they've got us surrounded," Allen commented.

Burt's eyes bugged. He had thought that they were up against a singular creature or at least had hoped that was the case.

"Frag," Burt muttered. "You got a plan?"

Allen shook his head. "Not really."

"Then I suggest we get out of here," Burt winced, shrugging off his backpack. He didn't want its weight slamming against him when it came time for them to run again.

"You sure you're going to be able to make it?" Allen glared at him.

"I'll make it," Burt snarled.

The two of them took off at a full out run, sprinting through the jungle heading for where the rest of the platoon should be. Burt was having a hard time keeping up but kept pushing himself on.

From seemingly out of nowhere, a creature leaped down out of a tree into their path. It landed only a few yards ahead of Allen. The thing stood over six feet tall as it rose up to its full height, standing on two legs like a man. Covered in brownish hair, the creature was a mass of rippling muscles as it charged at Allen. Its glowing yellow eyes were full of primal rage and its black lips parted in a snarl that showed razor-like teeth. Allen whipped up his M14. The rifle roared on full auto. Such bursts were nearly impossible to aim and rarely used but, in this instance, it was the best possible thing Allen could have done. The beast caught the full force of the burst at point blank range. The bullets carved up the flesh of its chest, punching through its ribs to leave gaping exit holes in the creature's back. The beast was dead before its toppling form even collapsed onto the ground.

"Frag!" Allen shouted, taking a step back from the dead thing on the jungle floor in front of him.

"They're in the trees!"

"What the hell are they?" Burt asked, not really expecting Allen to answer him.

The shrieks and cries around them grew louder, closing in from all sides.

"Get out of the way!" Allen yelled, shoving Burt to the side to clear his line of fire at the monster which came bursting out of the trees. His M14 roared again on full auto until it clicked empty. The monster took a dozen rounds and went down, flopping over sideways onto the muddy ground. Somehow, the creature was still alive. Its right hand lashed out, grabbing Burt's ankle as he was the closer of the two soldiers to where it lay. Burt screamed, nails tearing open his flesh, as he wrenched his ankle free of the beast's clutching grasp. Allen had ejected his rifle's spent magazine. He slammed a fresh one into the weapon as Allen put a round from his M21 into the dying beast's skull. The backside of its head burst apart in a shower of gore.

More of the ape-like creatures were almost upon them.

"You go!" Burt snapped at Allen. "There's no reason for us both to die out here."

Burt was surprised when Allen didn't listen to

him. From the look that the stone cold killer wore, Allen wasn't about to leave him behind. Burt had to change his mind.

"Someone has to warn the rest of the platoon," Burt spat. "We both know that between my back and ankle, I ain't going to make it."

Allen reluctantly nodded, acknowledging that the sniper was right. An ape thing burst from the trees right on top of them. Burt spun to face it, firing his M21. The shot smashed into the center of the ape thing's chest. The ape thing was dead but its momentum carried it on into Burt who was knocked over with the creature on top of him. Grunting, Burt rolled the dead ape creature off of him. Allen was already on the move. He caught a last glimpse of the killer disappearing into the jungle and hoped Allen would make it back.

Burt hobbled onto his feet, steadying his rifle and knowing he was about to die. There were just too many of the ape things. He had been lucky so far. They were so fast and fierce, Burt figured he should have been dead already. He was grateful he had discarded his backpack. It would have limited his movement, especially with his injuries. His plan was to buy time for Allen by drawing as many of the ape things as he could to him. And it sure as hell seemed to be working as he looked around. He could see at least five more of the creatures charging through the trees. Burt opened up, popping off shot after shot, only half aiming each. For every shot that hit, another buried itself into the wood of the trees that were providing some cover to the beasts as they closed in. One ape creature wailed as a round blew a chunk of flesh from its shoulder. Another died as a bullet shredded the soft tissue of its throat, sending blood spraying out from the mess it had become.

The first ape creature reached Burt. The sniper swung his rifle around towards it. His finger squeezed the weapon's trigger just as the beast lashed out, knocking it aside. The rifle boomed, spitting a round into the trunk of the tree near the two of them. Splinters flew into both Burt and the ape creature. The beast, ramped up on rage, didn't even seem to feel the splinters as they struck it. Burt wasn't as lucky. Splinters flew into his right cheek, imbedding themselves into it. He screamed in pain. The ape creature gave him no chance to recover. It grabbed hold of the rifle's barrel as Burt unconsciously righted it. Metal whined and creaked as the beast bent the barrel upwards before yanking the weapon out of Burt's hands.   There was a crack of bone as blood splattered. Two of Burt's fingers were torn away along with his M21. The rifle spun through the air, disappearing into the trees. Burt staggered as the ape creature took a swing at him. Only blind luck saved him from losing his head to the blow which surely would have severed his head from his shoulders had it made contact. Blood was pouring from his injured gun hand.   Weaponless, Burt knew he couldn't fight the ape creature. The thing could easily tear him limb from limb. His only hope was to try to make a run for it. Burt whirled around, trying to flee.   As he did, Burt found himself staring into the snarling face of another ape creature. One of its hands flashed outwards. The beast's claws were the last thing Burt ever saw as they raked his eyes from their sockets. Screaming, Burt dropped to his knees, reaching up with both hands to cover his empty eye sockets as blood streamed down his cheeks.   He felt oversized hands take hold of his head. With a quick jerk, there was a sharp cracking noise as the beast snapped his neck.

****

Allen moved as fast as he could through the

trees. He had no idea just how many of the ape-like beasts were chasing after him or how many others might be waiting somewhere up ahead. Burt's screams had fallen silent in the distance behind him. Allen hadn't really gotten a chance to get to know the sniper but he'd seemed like, not just a professional, but a nice guy too. Despite his rep, Burt had treated him like any other soldier and that spoke volumes about the sniper's character. Allen didn't blame folks for being scared of him, he knew exactly what he was and wasn't ashamed of it. There were soldiers like him in every war, people who loved what they did.

Whatever these things were, Allen didn't give a crap. They died just like everything else and that was enough to know about them as far as he was concerned. He had a fresh magazine in his M14 and figured he was ready for them. As he ran, Allen didn't just keep an eye on the trees ahead and around him, he scanned the limbs of the trees above him too. The ape creatures had gotten the drop on him once by dropping out of a tree and never would again.

An ape creature came screeching through the trees to his right. It didn't make any kind of attempt to take him by surprise. Yellow eyes burning with rage and black lips parted in a furious snarl, the beast made the mistake of thinking he'd be easy prey. Allen almost smiled as he swung his M14 up to target the thing. Not wanting to risk a full auto burst for fear of expending too much ammo, Allen aimed each of his shots as his rifle cracked three times in rapid succession. Whether the beast somehow sensed his first shot coming and managed to dodge it or just luck, Allen's first shot missed. His second didn't. The round dug into the beast's right arm. The ape creature shrieked in pain, increasing its speed instead of backing off as his third shot snapped its head back atop its neck, returning the beast to whatever nightmarish hell had given birth to it. Allen heard more of the beasts closing in on him. Looking over his shoulder, he saw a pack of them led by a creature larger than the others with it. The larger ape creature looked to be close to eight feet tall.

"Frag me," Allen muttered. There was no way in hell he was letting that thing get any closer. His left hand reached to yank a grenade from his belt, his thumb extracting its pin. Allen lobbed the grenade at the pack of charging monsters. It landed directly in their path, detonating there. The blast shredded the legs of the largest ape creature that was ahead of the others as shrapnel flew into both it and those behind it. Allen didn't stick around to see if the blast had killed all three of the creatures. He started running again, pushing his body to its limits. The rest of the platoon was still a long way away.

As he ran, Allen saw another ape creature coming after him. It was up in the trees, swinging and bounding from one to the other with impossible speed. The thing wasn't just gaining on him, it was almost already on him. Allen zagged to the left, darting around the trunk of a tree, as the beast leaped into it above him. He was ready for the creature as it leaped out of the tree, downward, at him. This time, he did let loose with a fully automatic burst of fire from his M14 that met the beast while it was still in the air. Bullets pummeled and ripped at the creature. Allen hurled himself out of the path of the beast's flight at the last moment. Its mangled body thudded into the ground where he had been standing. Out of spite, Allen kicked the thing's still twitching corpse. He had emptied his weapon into it. Allen let his M14 fall from his hands. There was another creature coming at him that was already too close to run from. The things were so fast that running wouldn't make much difference anyway. The creature would just overtake him if he tried. His best bet was to stand his ground and deal with the monster right here and now. It was the only other one that he could see or hear. Allen hoped it was the last of the things he was going to have to deal with. Taking a deep breath to steady himself, Allen drew his Ka-Bar 9140. His knuckles were white from how tightly he gripped the weapon's hilt below its seven-inch blade. Allen knew he was only going to get one shot at stopping the beast before it tore him apart. He saw almost a confused look in the monster's eyes as it closed on him as if it couldn't understand why he wasn't trying to run from it.

Allen waited, letting the beast come right at him. As it reached him, the ape creature took a swing at him, balled up fist lashing out at the side of his head. Allen ducked the blow and came up, driving the seven-inch blade of his knife into the monster's throat. He gave the knife a hard, rough twist. The beast's raging cries changed into a sickening gurgling as Allen wrenched his Ka-Bar free and threw himself sideways. The ape creature stumbled backwards instead of continuing after him. Blood was flowing in rivers down the length of its body, staining the thick brown of its chest red. There was fear in the beast's eyes as it seemed to realize that he'd just killed it. Allen's right hand rose up and behind his head. As it snapped forward, Allen threw his Ka-Bar at the creature. The blade spun end over end through the air to bury itself in the center of the beast's head. The ape creature collapsed, the hilt of his Ka-Bar protruding outward above its face. Allen held back, watching the beast thrash about in its death throes. When it was finally still, Allen walked over and pulled his knife free. He wiped its blade clean on the leg of his pants but didn't return the knife to its sheath.

The jungle was still and quiet around him. There was no sign that more of the ape creatures were coming for him. Allen took a deep breath again and got his nerves under control. He picked up his discarded M14 and slung it onto his shoulder by its strap. After another careful look around, Allen got moving, as silently as he could. Allen had to reach the rest of the platoon as quickly as he could. If they stumbled onto these ape creatures without knowing they were out here, it would likely be a bloodbath that they wouldn't survive.

****

Major Callen took stock of the situation around him. Most of the platoon was taking this chance to get some rest as he had intended them to. There were a few though who looked on edge either from the whacko encounter last night or merely being so far out in an area where the Viet Cong might just be building up forces for an all out attack. Sergeant Giffen and Corporal Dixon were at the edge of the clearing that the platoon had secured. With them were the Henry brothers who had apparently already returned from their recon run into the jungle. Callen took the brothers' early return as a bad sign. He started towards the four of them, rubbing at his back. Sleeping on the jungle floor always messed with it though. For him, there was just no getting used to it.

"Hey, Major!" Larry called to him in greeting, a wicked grin on the big man's face. The muscles of his arms were bulging as he held his M-60 braced against his right thigh. Harry, the younger of the two, looked happy too.

"These grunts actually brought us back some good news," Sergeant Giffen shook his head. "Can you believe that?"

"About time we caught a break," Corporal Dixon agreed.

"What's the news?" Callen asked.

Before anyone could answer him, Sergeant Giffen said, "Forgive me for saying it, sir, but you look like utter crap. You okay?"

"Sergeant," Callen said sharply. "Look around. It was a rough night for everybody."

"Got that right," Harry laughed. "But the good news is we found a village out there."

Callen cocked an eyebrow. "Inhabited?"

Larry shook his head. "Not that we could tell. We didn't go into it. Figured it was best to check in with you first, sir."

"Good call on that," Callen smiled.

"Thought the place might be a trap," Harry nodded, "but if it's not. . ."

"Then we can sure as hell use it," Callen said.

If the village was abandoned, it very well could serve as a base camp for them as they searched for the other missing platoons. Somewhere to hole up like that would be a huge thing to have. Of course, they were going to have to check it out first but the thought of the place being clear gave Callen hope. After last night, he really wanted out of the jungle. Right now, no matter what precautions they took, the truth was that they were exposed. Things could take a bad turn quickly if they ran into trouble with nowhere to fall back to.

"You two, go get some rest," Callen ordered the Henry brothers.

"Yes sir," they barked together and headed into the clearing where the rest of the platoon was.

"What are you thinking?" Dixon asked.

Callen sighed. "That this place might just be too good to be true."

"But we are going to check it out?" Giffen said.

Callen nodded. "We have to. It's too good a chance to find somewhere more secure than out here to pass up."

"Copy that," Dixon chuckled.

"What about the other recon team?" Callen turned to Giffen.

"They're not back yet," the sergeant told him. "But then, they aren't supposed to be yet. Those two just showed up early because of what they found out there."

"You're thinking of heading straight on to that village, aren't you?" Dixon flashed a wry grin.

"I think that would be best." Callen reached into his pocket, getting out a cigarette. He lit it up and sucked in a huge draw from it, breathing out the smoke slowly, savoring its flavor.

"I thought you gave those up," Giffen huffed.

"You thought wrong," Callen laughed. "As to your question, Corporal, yes, I am thinking every second we spend here, we're losing daylight. Best to get to that village with the sun still up. God only knows what may be waiting for us there. I'd rather find out before it gets dark."

"Can't argue with that," Giffen spat onto the jungle floor.

"But aren't we kind of stuck here waiting on Burt and Allen to get back?" Dixon shrugged.

"Burt may not be the tracker that Sheen is but I'm pretty sure he'll be able to follow us," Giffen pointed out. "The guy ain't no slouch."

"Are we really talking about this?" Dixon protested. "We can't just. . ."

"Last time I checked, I was in command here, Corporal," Callen cut him off.

Dixon was taken aback by Callen. It wasn't like him to be so cold and hard.

"Sorry, sir," Dixon frowned.

"We'll give them another half hour to make it back," Callen's voice was calmer. He hadn't really meant to snap at Dixon like he had. The weird feeling in his gut about something being off with things out here had gotten the better of him. "If they haven't made it in by then, they should be able to find us like Giffen said. Besides, it'll take us that long to let the Henry brothers catch their breath and get everyone moving."

The next half hour ticked by like an eternity to Callen. He finished his cigarette and smoked two more while the others who weren't on watch got ready to move out. Callen paced about, unable to keep still. He was eager to get to the village that the Henry brothers had located. The sun was high in the sky but soon it would start to go down and Callen wanted to reach the village long before then. As it was, they were going to have to double time it in order make that happen which made them even more exposed to attack by. . . Callen, scowling, lit up yet another smoke. It wasn't the Viet Cong that had entered his mind but images from his dark dream about monsters in the jungle. He could feel the glare of animal-like, yellow eyes burning into the depths of his very soul. Callen shuddered and then tossed what remained of his cigarette onto the ground and smashed it out with his boot.

"You ready?" Corporal Dixon asked, walking up to him.

"As I ever will be," Callen sighed. "Let's get

going."

Sergeant Giffen and Sheen took point again. Burt and Allen had never returned. Callen hoped that Burt could really track them to the village they were headed for. If not, he was sure that they'd be found after the village was secured and set up as a base camp for the platoon to expand their search from. As yet, there hadn't been any sort of sign at all of the other platoons that had gone missing. The men all knew that they were supposed to be looking for such signs but Callen doubted any of them were. Whether they were showing it or not, Callen could tell they were all just as rattled as he was.

A few hours later, the platoon came upon the village that the Henry brothers had found. The platoon fanned out, approaching it cautiously from all sides. The plan was to move in hard and fast, not giving the Viet Cong a chance to spring their trap if there was one.

Callen burst from the trees, his M-14 clutched tight, and ready for action. Corporal Dixon and Sergeant Giffen were leading other squads into the village from the east and west. Callen's eyes swept over the scene in front of him. The village was little more than a collection of primitive huts.

Scattered everywhere on the ground between them were the rotting bodies of the people who looked to have once lived within them. There were no signs of the Viet Cong or anything alive. Maggots crawled over the decaying corpses. Callen covered his mouth and nose with one hand, keeping his M-14 aimed ahead of him with the other.

"Clear!" Corporal Dixon's voice shouted from the east.

"Clear here, too!" Sergeant Giffen called out as he and his squad came in from the other side of the village.

Everyone in the platoon was reacting to the mess they had just stumbled onto. Someone. . . or something…had massacred everyone who lived here. Every single person, man, woman, and child. Some of the men in the platoon fell to their knees vomiting, others simply gawked at the carnage in shock and horror. These men were hardened soldiers but they were still human.

"Fragging Hell!" Larry Henry yelled. "Something's been eating these bastards!"

"We're in a jungle, you idiot," Harry shouted. "What ya think is gonna happen to bodies left out like this?"

Sergeant Giffen shut both of them up, "Keep

your voices down! We don't know if we're alone here or not yet!"

"Everybody fan out. I want this place secured A.S.A.P," Callen barked.

Seconds ticked by like hours to Callen as his men spread out inside the village. It was clear though. There was no one in the place but the dead. He looked up to see Corporal Dixon emerge from one of the village's huts.

"Major," Corporal Dixon got his attention, motioning to him.

Callen walked along the center of the village, stepping around some corpses and over others. The stench was horrid. He was holding it together though and not surrendering to his guts wanting to empty their contents.

"What is it, Corporal?" Callen asked.

"There's something in that hut you need see, sir," Dixon told him.

Callen looked around making as sure as he could that the others had finished securing the village. Sergeant Giffen appeared to have things well in hand. There was no reason for him not to take the time to see what Dixon had found.

Sheen and Fox were waiting inside the hut as Dixon led Callen into it. Fox looked like he'd rather be anywhere else. Sheen was chewing on a mouthful of tobacco and frowning. Towards the hut's far wall were three bodies. Callen gawked at the closest of them in disbelief. What was left of the man was clearly wearing U.S. Army fatigues and an M16 lay on the dirt floor near him. There were spent shell casings everywhere inside the hut. Light spilled inside from a dozen places where bullets had pierced the hut's walls. The other two bodies were Vietnamese children, one male, one female.

"Guy put up a hell of a fight, Major," Sheen said. "That's easy to see. What don't make sense though is why the poor bastard was protecting those children."

Major Callen didn't have to ask how the soldier had died. The entire front of his face was caved in leaving nothing more than a rotting hole of broken bone and bloody flesh. Something had smashed it in with a single blow. The children's bodies were far worse off. Both of them were missing limbs and Callen could see where chunks of meat had been ripped away from their bodies.

"Those are tooth marks," Sheen pointed at a mangled portion of the young girl's body. "You see 'em, sir?"

"I see them," Callen sighed.

"Ain't no animals around these parts except maybe a tiger that would do something like this," Sheen commented. "But. . ."

Callen turned to look at the hut's door behind him. "A tiger never would have made it in here with him blasting away with his M16 like that."

"Exactly," Sheen nodded. "Like I said, ain't nothing about this here that makes sense."

"The people here. . . they were apparently just people, farmers based on the fields out there behind this place," Dixon shrugged. "And this guy. . ."

Dixon nudged the dead soldier's body with the tip of his boot. "What he was doing here is as big of a mystery as whatever killed him is."

"This crap is all messed up," Sheen shook his head.

"Tell me about it," Fox agreed, still looking sickly.

"An American soldier protecting folks like these isn't unheard of, ya know," Dixon commented. "That bandage on his upper right arm makes me think he was hurt already. The villagers must have either found and carried him here or he found the place on his own and they gave him shelter. That would fully explain why he was trying to protect them if he was in their debt."

"I don't suppose it matters," Sheen huffed. "Dead is dead. Ain't none of them folks coming back."

"Sheen's right," Major Callen spoke up. "We've been blessed in finding this place to use as a basecamp but there's a hell of a lot of work to do to get it in shape. Get these bodies outside with the others."

"Yes sir," Corporal Dixon said.

Sergeant Giffen met him as Callen emerged from the hut. "The place is clear. Guess it's ours if we want it."

"We do." Callen looked around. "We're going to have do something with the bodies though."

"Can't just burn them," Sergeant Giffen frowned. "The smoke. . ."

"Mass grave then," Callen ordered. "Get some of the men to work on that. I want the rest setting up some surprises in the jungle for anything that comes our way tonight but don't let any of them go out there alone to do it."

"Expecting trouble?" Sergeant Giffen asked.

"Aren't you?" Callen quipped.

"Always," Sergeant Giffen snorted.

The sergeant hurried away, barking orders at the closest soldiers of the platoon leaving Major Callen to his thoughts as he wandered around the ruins of the village. Some of the huts were literally smashed apart. His worries about exactly what had happened here only continued to grow. Callen's instincts told him that big trouble was headed their way after the sun set. He glanced up at the gathering clouds above. The sun had started its descent but was still high in the sky.

Eventually, Callen found a spot to sit. He lit up a smoke and shrugged off his pack, placing it on the ground in front of him. Callen rummaged through its contents hunting for something to eat. Opening up a can of "turkey loaf", his nose curled at its smell. He stared at the meat in the can. There was nothing attractive about it. It stunk almost as bad as the dead bodies scattered throughout the village. Disgusted, Callen tossed the can of turkey loaf aside. Callen opened up his bread ration, taking a bite out of a hardtack biscuit. It dried out his mouth so he sat down his cigarette long enough to screw the lid off his canteen and took a swig.

There was still no sign of the other team Giffen and Dixon had sent out. Callen hoped that Burt and Allen were okay. He didn't know Allen, outside of what was contained in his personnel file, but he knew that Burt was one hell of a professional. Callen hadn't liked leaving them out there to fend for themselves. He took another bite of his biscuit, finishing it, and then got to his feet as he saw Sergeant Giffen approaching him.

"This place is as secure as we can make it," Sergeant Giffen reported. "We got trip wires in the woods and several guys spread out on watch. Corporal Dixon and his group are still working on that grave. Shouldn't take them much longer."

The Henry brothers and others had already been dragging the corpses into a pile next to the grave that was being dug. Major Callen didn't want to think about just how many bodies there were in that pile. . . dozens to be sure, some of them far too young to have met death the way they had. That was war and its horrors seemed to know no end.

Sergeant Giffen looked as if he had more to say.

"What is it, Giffen?" Callen asked.

"All those bodies, every one of them. . . they've been gnawed on, sir," the sergeant answered. "I get that there are plenty of big cats out there, heard that there's bears too, but, Major. . .I don't think for a second it was anything normal that killed and ate on these villagers."

"I don't think so either, Giffen," Callen said. "I think whatever it was that we ran into out there did this but I'll be damned if I know what it was."

Neither of them spoke for a moment.

"There are stories of ape creatures in these jungles," Sergeant Giffen said.

"You're talking about Rock Apes," Callen was scowling as he spoke. "I've heard those stories too. Never gave them any credence until now."

"You're not thinking that. . ." Sergeant Giffen started.

"I hate to admit it but yeah, I am," Callen sighed.

"That's crazy," Sergeant Giffen huffed and then caught himself. "Sorry, sir, I didn't mean any disrespect."

"It's okay, Giffen," Callen shrugged. "It is crazy but that doesn't mean it's not true. God only knows what we're dealing with out here but at this point, I think we've got more than the Viet Cong to worry about."

"That's why you wanted us to get to this village so badly," Sergeant Giffen commented.

"It's not much safer than the jungle, sure, but the trees are cut back around most of it. If there is something not right coming for us, at least we'll have a chance of getting some warning," Callen explained. "Guess we'll be finding out, maybe more than we want to, after the sun sets. Gonna need you to make sure the men are ready for anything."

"You can bet on that, sir," Sergeant Giffen promised.

****

Night fell over the village. The light of the stars and moon were mostly obscured by rain clouds that continued to build. The jungle around the place was filled with trip wires. Most of them were rigged to launch warning flares skyward but a few were actually grenades. Callen wished they had somehow brought mines with them. He would have ordered them deployed too. Anything that would add to the security of the perimeter of the village was what they needed right now. Thankfully, the jungle was pushed back a good bit around in most directions, a solid dozen yards or more of cleared ground which anything coming at them would have to cross.

The platoon did have two M-60s, one belonging to the older Henry brother and the other carried by a private named Hammel. Major Callen made sure both of them were on watch with another trooper supporting each of them. A few other soldiers were spread out on watch around the village as well. Major Callen could only hope that it would be enough if the Viet Cong or anything else showed themselves during the night. Sergeant Giffen had done his best to convince Callen to get some sleep but that wasn't happening. Callen had picked a spot in the center of the village and sat there, leaning against the side of a hut, waiting for things to go to hell. His instincts told him that they would sooner rather than later.

Sergeant Giffen was awake as well. He'd assigned himself as Hammel's fire team support. Giffen had traded out the M14 he'd been carrying during the day for a pump action shotgun. Giffen didn't smoke often but tonight he was longing for a cigarette. He didn't give into the craving though, instead finding a thick piece of weed which protruded from his mouth as his teeth worked on its end. Giffen was greatly concerned about the major, worried that he was pushing himself too far. He'd never seen Callen so on edge before.

"Sarge, you gotta stop stressing," Hammel nudged him in the shoulder. "This ain't the first rodeo for most of us. We're gonna get through this one too."

Sergeant Giffen grunted. "Sure thing. Now keep your fragging attention on the trees."

"Just what is it you think is out there, sir?" Hammel asked carefully, his voice level and calm. "We ain't seen any sign of the Viet Cong since those copters dumped us. And this Rock Ape talk that's going around. . . well, that's crap, Sarge."

"Ya think?" Sergeant Giffen frowned at the blue-eyed kid.

"I mean, I heard about them Rock Ape things in stories but they were just that, sir. . . stories," Hammel continued. "I've never seen an animal in real life that was dumb enough to attack an entire group of armed men. That just don't make no sense, sir."

"I hear ya," Sergeant Giffen nodded. "Now shut up and that's an order."

"Yes sir," Hammel responded and went back to staring into the shadows of the jungle's tree line.

On the far side of the village, Fox and Stu were having a similar talk.

"I've heard enough about fragging apes already,

Fox, so unless you got something else to talk about, just keep it quiet, okay?" Stu warned the handsome man sitting next to him.

Fox laughed, flashing a wry grin. "I know what we can talk about, buddy, and that's what we're gonna do when we get out of this hell. Me? I am gonna find some nice looking Donut Dollies and shack up with them for the entire time."

Stu shifted uncomfortably where he sat. "More than one, huh?"

"What? You judging me with those Texan values again, man?" Fox cut his eyes at Stu.

"I don't think they're Texan values, Fox. I just don't understand why any guy would ever want more than one girl," Stu countered.

"Whooeh, Stu," Fox whooped more loudly than he likely should have. "As my old man used to tell me, don't knock it until you tried it."

"You're a very sick man, Fox," Stu shook his head.

"Yeah, well. . ." Fox started to argue back but Stu held up a hand telling him to keep quiet.

"Something's moving out there," Stu said.

Fox squinted at the distant trees. He couldn't see squat in them.

"You sure?" Fox whispered. "I don't see

anything."

"Over there," Stu pointed. "You see what I'm seeing?"

Fox looked at the spot Stu indicated. There was something that seemed to be glowing in the darkness. Then it finally clicked in his mind what he was looking at. The glow was coming from a pair of bright, yellow eyes which were staring back at them from the jungle.

"Crap, man," Fox muttered. "That's creepy as hell."

"What do you think it is?" Stu asked.

"Frag me if I know," Fox answered. "Sure as hell ain't no Viet Cong soldier."

"Has to be some sort of animal but why is it just sitting there?" Stu said. "It's like the thing is just watching us, waiting for something."

Fox took aim at the thing in the shadows with his M14. "Tell you what, man, let's just light that fragger up and find out what it is later."

Stu reached over, placing a hand on Fox's rifle, shoving its barrel downwards.

"We light that thing up and it's just some dumb animal that we shouldn't be worried about, the sergeant will have our heads, buddy," Stu cautioned.

"Look at those eyes, man," Fox argued. "Ain't nothing right about them. I am not just going to sit here and keep looking at them. What if that thing out there is measuring us up, just waiting on the right moment to make its move?"

"Come on, buddy," Stu wasn't honestly sure if he was trying to reassure Fox or himself that thing wasn't really a threat. "It's just some animal."

"Frag that crap, man." Fox pulled his rifle out of Stu's grip, taking aim at the glowing eyes in the trees again. His finger tightened on the M14's trigger. The rifle cracked, bucking against his shoulder as it fired. Then everything went to hell. Fox couldn't tell if he had hit his target or not. The glowing yellow eyes had withdrawn into the darkness. All around the village a cacophony of howls and inhuman cries rose up. Dozens of hulking, ape-like creatures came bursting from the trees towards the village. Trip wires went off sending flares streaking into the night sky, illuminating the horror of the monsters' charge. The few grenades on trip wires detonated as well, the light of their explosions flashing brightly along the village's perimeter. Fox had just loosed the fury of hell upon the platoon and he knew it. Several of the ape things were racing across the cleared ground between the village and jungle towards his and Stu's position.

"Take the fraggers out!" Stu screamed. "If they reach us, we're dead, man!"

Fox and Stu poured fire into the approaching creatures. Rounds hammered into their chests, upper thighs, and arms as the things loped towards them with seemingly impossible speed. One of the creatures finally collapsed, its body riddled with bullet holes but. . .it was just one. The others were taking everything Stu and Fox were throwing at them and still advancing.

One of the larger, faster ape creatures flung itself through the air, landing directly in front of Stu and Fox. Stu screamed like a startled schoolgirl despite all his Texan toughness. The beast lashed out with a powerful swipe of a clawed hand that sent Stu's rifle flying out of his grip and knocked him sideways. Fox fired point blank into the beast, his rifle cracking over and over in rapid succession as fast as his finger could work its trigger. The bullets thudded into the beast's chest, punching holes through the thick muscles there. The ape creature staggered backwards as Fox adjusted his aim. His next three shots struck the beast in its lower jaw and throat. The thing's roars became squeals of pain as it reeled away from Fox.

Stu had gotten back to his feet and was sprinting towards where his M14 lay several feet away. He'd almost reached the weapon when an ape creature came bounding into him. The beast rammed into his side. Ribs gave way, popping and cracking inside him, from the force of the impact. Blood flew from Stu's mouth as the ape creature closed its massive arms about his body and hugged him to its chest, crushing him against it.

Fox saw Stu die but had no time to do anything about it. Another two of the ape creatures were bounding up to him, black lips parted in fierce snarls, yellow eyes burning with primal rage. Fox could hear the rest of the platoon in the village waking up and getting into the action as more of the creatures rushed past his position. The first of the two creatures got close enough to engage Fox. He quickly backpedaled, narrowly avoiding a hair-covered, balled up fist. It whooshed through the air of the spot where he'd been standing. The barrel of his M14 flashed as Fox fired a round into the monster's face. Jaw bone broke, fragmenting and folding inward, as the bullet entered the monster, snapping its head back atop its neck. Fox let loose again before the beast could recover.

Another two rounds followed that first shot, hammering into the beast's head. One blew clean through it, an explosion of gore erupting from a bursting exit wound in the back of its skull. The beast collapsed, twitching.

The second ape creature reached Fox just as the first died at his feet. Fox jerked up his M14 to block the foul beast's raking claws as they swung towards him. Fox nearly lost his hold on the rifle. Not that it mattered. The rifle broke in two in his hands. Though it saved his life, the M14 was now useless, leaving him without a weapon. The ape creature roared. It was a deafening sound at such close range, hurting Fox's ears. Making the only move he could, Fox yanked the Ka-bar sheathed on his belt free from its scabbard. The beast never gave him the chance to use it, the thick fingers of its right hand catching and closing about his arm. With a single flick of its mighty wrist, the ape creature snapped Fox's forearm like a twig. Fox cried out in pain, looking down at the jagged white shards of bone protruding through the flesh of his mangled arm. His wailing was silenced as another blow from the beast removed Fox's head from his shoulders and sent it bouncing across the jungle floor behind him.

****

"Fragging hell!" Larry Henry shouted as flares soared skyward, lighting up the night, and dozens of hairy *things* came charging out of the trees. The creatures resembled apes but there was something much more ferocious about them, something more human too. Their eyes burned yellow even in the glow of flares above. They snarled and shrieked as they bounded across the cleared ground between the jungle and the edge of the village.

Harry, the older of the Henry brothers, didn't need anyone to tell him what to do. His M60 chattered, spitting ejected casings from its side, as he poured fire into the monsters. The high-powered rounds cut the first three of the beasts to shreds. The other beasts paid no attention to the big gun's roar or their dying brethren. They kept their course, pressing forward.

Larry snatched up his Thumper, fumbling a grenade into its chamber. He clicked the weapon shut, swinging it up to face the charging creatures. The fastest of the beasts were already too close in for Larry to target without risking blowing his own butt to Hell too. He fired the M79's grenade at those behind the first wave that were still emerging from the jungle. The blast lit the night, sending shrapnel flying. One of the beasts screeched as its side was ripped open in a bloody mess of gore. Another lost a leg to the blast and toppled, rolling through the grass, carried forward by its own momentum. The third of the beasts within the range of the blast took shrapnel in its left arm and shoulder. That arm now dangled limply at the beast's side.

M60 fire continued to hammer the charging beasts as they drew closer to the Henry brothers and Henry saw that his belt of ammo was almost gone. Thankfully, most of the beasts coming at them were dead. The heavy weapon had done a hell of a job chopping the stupid animals up. The cleared ground between the tree line and the village was littered with dead beasts. Harry was still mentally patting himself on the back when one of the creatures snatched up a rock and heaved it at him. He didn't have a chance in dodging the projectile. The rock struck Henry smack in the middle of his forehead. A crunching sound filled his ears as his vision went all blurry and the world spun around him. Henry reached up to touch where the rock had hit him. He jerked his fingers away in horror from what he felt there. They were drenched in blood. The world spun faster becoming even more blurred as his brain began to shut down. Harry slumped forward onto his M60 and lay there, his body spasming every few seconds.

"Harry!" Larry wailed as he saw the rock hit his older brother. Racing to him, Larry rolled Harry over and recoiled in disgust. The rock had opened up Harry's skull. His brain matter, mixed with blood, leaked from the gaping wound. Larry was caught off guard as one of the ape creatures leaped onto him. He screamed as his grenade launcher went bouncing out of his hands and the full force of the ape thing's weight smashed him into the ground. Larry's right arm snapped at its elbow and the shin of his left leg broke, bone splintering beneath the flesh covering it. The ape creature rose up, towering above him, as its legs straddled his body. Raising clasped, hair-covered hands above its head, the beast brought them down in a blow that shattered Larry's ribs. He gasped as his own bones pierced his lungs. . . and then there was only blackness.

Sergeant Giffen couldn't believe the crap storm that had just been let loose around them as he and Hammel fought to hold back the beasts racing out of the jungle towards the village. Flares lit the sky and there had been raging gunfire heard from all of the other watch positions. The fragging animals had come just like Major Callen had predicted that they would. Deep down, Sergeant Giffen had hoped that the major would be wrong about the beasts. Still, he hoped that at least here in this village, they stood a chance of keeping beasts from tearing them all apart.

"Keep fragging firing!" Sergeant Giffen shouted over the roar of Hammel's M60 and the thunderous booming of his own shotgun. He worked its pump, chambering another round as one of the beasts flanked their position, coming in at them from outside Hammel's field of fire. Spinning to meet it, the barrel of his shotgun flashed as he squeezed the weapon's trigger. His shot slammed into the ape creature's stomach. Guts exploded outward from where the heavy slug he'd fired entered. The beast doubled over in pain, its snarls changing to a pathetic whimpering noise. Sergeant Giffen didn't give the beast a chance to recover. He worked the pump of his shotgun, chambering a fresh round, before sending the beast back to whatever Hell the thing had crawled out of with a second shot that reduced the top of its skull to an exploding mass of bone fragments and gore.

Behind him, the sound of heavy M60 fire had fallen silent. In the next instant, Sergeant Giffen heard Hammel screaming. He whirled around to see the private lifted up by one of the hulking monsters. The beast smashed Hammel back down onto the ground with such force that every bone in the man's body seemed to break. As if that wasn't enough, the beast stomped Hammel with one of its huge feet, over and over in a violent rage. Sergeant Giffen put a round into the beast's side sending it stumbling away from the bloody mess that once had been Hammel.

Sergeant Giffen tossed away his now empty shotgun knowing with the beasts as close to him as they were that he'd never be able to reload it before they were on him. He wore a 1911 pistol holstered on his hip and drew it as he abandoned his position and ran like hell into the village. Sergeant Giffen was met by others of the platoon rushing forward to support him. Sheen and another soldier named Warren held their fire until he was past them before they opened up on the snarling monsters following in his wake.

Sheen and Warren didn't have a prayer of stopping the monsters. There were too many, coming too fast. One of the apes charged directly into Warren, taking a half dozen rounds from his M14 in its chest. They weren't enough to stop it though. The beast got its hands on Warren, clawing away half of his face with a single swipe of a clawed hand while its other hand rammed into the middle of his body. Sergeant Giffen saw the blood-covered fist that punched out of Warren's back after going all the way through him.

The first beast to reach Sheen met more than it bargained for as M14 fire pounded into its face and neck. Its corpse dropped to the ground, flopping about. Sheen was no idiot and knew he wouldn't be as lucky with the next monster. Sergeant Giffen watched as Sheen tried to turn and make a run for it. A hair-covered hand erupted through the center of his chest, clutching his still beating heart as blood exploded like vomit, spraying out of Sheen's mouth. Sergeant Giffen turned and kept running. He skidded to a halt, frozen by what he saw ahead of him. The ape creatures had made it into the village and a massacre was taking place in front of his eyes.

****

Major Callen was alert and ready, sitting in the

center of the village, burning through one cigarette after another, as the attack started. Now there was utter chaos all around him. The ape creatures had broken through the village's defensive lines and were seemingly everywhere. Only God knew how many of these things there were. . . too many, that was for fragging sure.

He took a look about and saw what was left of his platoon being taken apart, unable to hold their ground, with nowhere to fall back to. Major Callen leaped to his feet, M14 swinging up to target a snarling monster that was bounding towards a private named Wandrey. Before Major Callen could open fire, hands grabbed him from behind, dragging him into the hut he'd been sitting outside of. Major Callen ripped free of their hold on him, ramming the butt of his rifle into the gut of his attacker. He heard an all too human grunt of pain, whirling around to see Lovecraft lying on the dirt floor with his hands clamped over his stomach.

"What the hell?" Major Callen yelled.

"Shut up!" Lovecraft sucked in enough breath to that much out as he grabbed Major Callen's legs and swept them out from under him. Callen landed on the floor next to the radio operator, paying the price for underestimating the geeky kid.

Lovecraft was on top of him with a hand clamped over his mouth faster than Callen would have thought possible. "We have to keep quiet, sir. Have to. This battle is lost and you know it."

Callen glared up into Lovecraft's terrified eyes, seriously thinking about bashing in the kid's brains but as he did, the roars and growls of the beasts outside the hut continued to grow in their intensity and volume. Lovecraft was just trying to keep them both alive and. . . frag it. . . the kid was right too. The moment the ape creatures had gotten into the village, the platoon's fate had been sealed. Callen made sure Lovecraft could see he had calmed down a bit as he eased the radio operator's hand from where it covered his mouth.

A cacophony of gunfire and screams could be heard from all around the hut Lovecraft had brought them into. The young radio operator's expression remained one of sheer terror. Callen couldn't blame him. They were in it deep. It was going to take a miracle for them to make it out of the village arrive. Callen was struggling with what his next move had to be. He wasn't the sort of officer who left men behind. Never had been. Nonetheless, Callen didn't have any choice right now. He was just one man. Attempting to save what was left of the platoon would simply be suicide. That was the cold hard truth and it wouldn't make a bit of difference to anyone if he died trying. There was duty and then was there was stupidity. A good soldier needed to know the difference and as much as it hurt him, Callen did. Lovecraft had made the right move and had at least saved them both for the moment. The ape creatures hadn't realized they were in the hut yet but that was sure to change and quickly too.

Lovecraft was watching him closely, waiting to see what he was going to do. Callen didn't have an answer, not a good one at any rate. They needed a way out. Just staying in the hut where they were was as much suicide as joining the battle outside.

"We can't stay here," Callen whispered.

Lovecraft, pale and scared to death, nodded.

Getting to his feet, Callen crept to the doorway of the hut, peeking outside. It was just as bad as he thought. Most of his men were already dead. There were a few holdouts, here and there, but they were fighting a purely desperate and defensive battle. . . and a losing one. Then Callen saw Corporal Dixon. . .

****

Corporal Dixon was screwed and knew it. He had his back to a hut with an M14 in each hand. Both rifles were blazing as he poured rounds into the beasts that were raging through the village. Dixon fired a trio of rounds that sent blood splattering out of an ape creature's ruptured throat. The thing's monstrous roaring silenced, the beast collapsed to the ground to be trampled by another beast behind it. Corporal Dixon broke from his position just as the beast got close enough to take a swing at him. Its fist smashed through the wall of the hut as he narrowly avoided the blow. Dixon sprinted away from the ape creature and the hut, leaving them behind him. As he ran, Dixon caught a glimpse of Major Callen in the doorway of another hut not too far away. He had to fight his instincts which told him to head straight for his C.O. Doing that would lead the beasts right to the major and anyone else who might be inside the hut with him, sealing their fate as much as his own.

There were three ape creatures bounding after Dixon and more beginning to turn their attention to him as he ran on through the village. The second he so much as slowed down, Dixon would be dead. Of course, as fast as the beasts were, that was going to happen sooner rather than later anyway. At best, his full out effort, was merely buying him a few more seconds of life. The night was dark. More clouds had rolled in and the heavens above let loose in a sudden deluge. Dixon felt it slicking his skin and soaking through his clothes almost instantly. He blinked drops of it from his eyes. Lightning flashed and a boom of thunder followed closely after it. The ground beneath his feet was mud in an instant. As his right foot came down with his next step, it slid from under him. Dixon lost his balance. Cursing, he splashed into the mud. The impact jarred Dixon, shaking him up. One of his M14s bounced out of his grip. He swung the other up and around at an ape creature that had gained on him more than the others. The rifle cracked in rapid succession as he worked its trigger. Each round he fired slammed into the monster but failed to drive it back. Whether the beast was just pushing through its pain or carried on by its own momentum didn't fragging matter. The ape creature wasn't stopping.

Something flashed in the darkness again only this time it wasn't lightning. The flash came from somewhere in the jungle beyond the village. An RPG streaked by Dixon and the beast he was engaged with. The grenade struck a nearby hut, detonating in a blinding blast of white fire. The hut erupted into flames despite the pouring rain. Someone out there had fired Willie Pete into the village and saved his life. The beast that had been on the verge of tearing his face off was caught as much by surprise as he was, only it went crazy at the sight of the unnatural flames. Dixon scrambled, slipping and sliding, to his feet. He was running again as another Willie Pete grenade flew into the village. This time, the grenade hit one of the ape creatures, setting its hair-covered body ablaze. The beast shrieked and howled, darting about wildly in blind rage and pain as it burned. Whoever was firing the Willie Pete grenades was either a genius or one fragging lucky bastard. A final grenade flew into the village, striking the mud and spreading Willie Pete across it in waves of rolling fire. The grenades broke the nerve of the ape creatures and sent them all retreating into the night.

Major Callen and the platoon's radio operator, Lovecraft, emerged from the hut they were taking cover in, racing towards him.

"Corporal!" the major shouted. "Get your ass in gear!"

Dixon realized they weren't heading for him at

all but rather towards the trees of the jungle in the direction that the grenades had come from. He changed his course, meeting up with Callen and Lovecraft.

Callen was the fastest of them, remaining well in the lead, as they raced out of the village. Crossing the section of cleared ground between it and the jungle, Callen glanced back, expecting to see at least some of the ape creatures hot on their heels but there weren't any. The fire had freaked out the monsters so badly, there was no sign of any of them now. There was however movement in the trees ahead of them. The barrel of Callen's rifle swung up but he stopped short of squeezing the trigger.

"Don't shoot!" a human voice shouted from the darkness amid the trees.

Callen and the others came to a stop just inside the tree line, gawking at the man in front of them.

"What?" Allen asked.

"We thought you were dead," Corporal Dixon managed to get out.

Allen looked as if he had come close to it. Most of his clothes were picked or torn by tree limbs and briars. Dried blood stained him nearly head to toe. There was a mad, feral edge to Allen's eyes. Clearly, Allen had been through hell out here while they were setting up inside the village. Just as Callen hoped though, Allen found his way to them. Callen wanted to ask him where Burt was but knew there was no time for such things.

"This way!" Allen barked at the three of them and then whirled about, charging deeper into the jungle.

****

The small group ran for what felt like hours. Maybe it was. Callen couldn't really tell. All he knew was how badly the muscles of his legs ached and his lungs burned. Lovecraft was barely staying on his feet. Hell, that was true of all of them except maybe Allen. If they made it back alive, Callen was going to make fragging sure the guy got some kind of medal.

Allen led them to a cave of all places. Callen and the others with him balked at entering it.

"It's clear," Allen assured them. "I holed up here for a bit earlier to get my bearings."

"How the hell do you know it's still clear now?" Dixon demanded.

"Sure, this cave used to be a home to those things out there," Allen waved a hand at the jungle around them. "But trust me, I'd wager it's been a long time since they've been back to it."

"Doesn't matter if it's clear or not," Callen barked. "We're going in. Everyone keep your guard up and weapons ready."

Allen entered the cave ahead of the others though Callen was close on his heels. The cave was much deeper than Callen would have thought possible. It opened up into a large central area with smaller tunnels branching out of it.

Something crunched under Callen's boots as Allen lit up the cave's interior with the beam of a flashlight. Callen nearly screamed like a little kid as he saw that what had made the noise beneath his feet was a layer of broken and gnawed upon bones which covered the entire floor of the cave.

"Frag me," Callen muttered.

"We need to get the hell out of here right now," Dixon shouted.

"Hold up," Allen ordered though he lacked the rank to truly give such a command. "There aren't any of those creatures here, man. I mean it. Take a closer look around. This place is old. It hasn't been used in a good while."

Dixon was glaring at Allen.

"There's no fresh crap in here," Allen pointed

out. "No smell of urine either. And look at the fragging bones. You can tell they've been where they are for a long time."

"He's right," Callen backed Allen up. "We should be safe here for a little while. If there were any of those creatures in here, we'd know it already."

Allen nodded, "I've checked out the side tunnels. All of them are dead ends. The mouth is the only way in or out of this cave. Cover it and the place is secure."

"On it," Dixon frowned, clearly still unhappy about the decision to stay but moved to do just as Allen as had suggested, taking up a firing position that allowed him a decent view of the area beyond the cave's mouth.

"I've got a lot of questions," Callen eyed Allen.

Allen shrugged. "Figured you did. Really there's not that much to it. Burt and I were attacked by those things. He didn't make it. Put up one hell of a fight though. Bought me time to get away. I ran for my life, heading back for the platoon's position, only to find all of you gone. Picking up your trail wasn't hard though. I started following it but the jungle is filled with those things. Ended up needing to find some cover for a bit and found this place. Stumbled on it honestly. Gave me time to get my head together."

"Like I said, I'm glad you made it," Callen assured him.

"There's more to my story than just that though," Allen said.

Callen raised an eyebrow. "Go on then."

"Before I caught up with you guys at the village, I found the bodies of Lieutenant Wagner's platoon."

"What?" Callen blurted out in shock. "Where?"

"Not far from here actually." Allen paused, taking in a breath and then asked, "You wouldn't happen to have a smoke would you, sir?"

"Sure," Callen produced his last, almost empty pack of cigarettes and handed it over to Allen.

He took one, lit up, and passed the pack back.

"Thanks," Allen said between taking heavy drags. "I needed this."

Callen simply nodded, waiting for Allen to get back to his story.

"Anyway, the lieutenant's platoon had been slaughtered, torn to pieces, and looked to have served as a meal for those creatures." Allen wore a disgusted expression on his face. "By my count, the apes or whatever you want to call them, killed them all but one. Someone made it out of that mess when it went down. Who knows if they're dead now or not?"

"I hear ya," Callen urged Allen on.

"I looted what I could of the platoon's gear that I thought would be useful and continued. That's where I got the Willie Pete," Allen told him. "I had no idea the stuff would screw with those things as bad as it did but frag, it sure sent them running, didn't it?"

"Yeah, it did," Callen agreed. "Do you have any left?"

"Got two more WP grenades, sir," Allen grinned.

"Good," Callen smiled. "Then maybe we've got a shot of making it out of here. Give me one of them."

Callen took the grenade Allen handed him, ramming it into his pocket.

Allen appeared doubtful but didn't challenge him on it. All of them were well aware that Lovecraft didn't have his radio pack with him. The kid had left it in the village. They couldn't call for extraction or any kind of support. It was going to be up to them to save their own arses or die out here.

"So that's it then?" Lovecraft asked, sounding hopeful that their nightmare was almost over. "We're really just heading home?"

"We know what happened to Lieutenant Wagner and his men and who did it now, too," Callen answered him. "That was our mission. There's no point sticking around any longer. What we need to focus on at this point is making sure we do get home and don't end up like Wagner's group did."

"Amen to that," Dixon said from his spot near the cave's mouth.

"Making it out won't be easy," Allen warned. "There are lot more of those ape things than you're likely thinking there are."

"There were dozens of them that came at us in the village," Callen said.

"Oh, there are more than dozens, sir," Allen shook his head. "Best I can tell, I'd put their number in the hundreds. This place is their turf. Most likely always has been until this war. Remember they took out a Viet Cong platoon too. To them, anything human is either a threat to their territory or prey. The village I'd guess was just beyond the edge of what those things claims as theirs and they hit it because of us and the Viet Cong then followed you back there to make sure you learned your lesson about coming into it."

"You're making them sound fragging smart of being just animals," Dixon snorted.

"Who said that they were just animals?" Lovecraft countered. "Those things have likely been around longer than men like us have. God only knows how long they've been around. Could be they're just as smart, maybe even smarter than we are, in their own way."

"We've underestimated them already and paid the price for it," Callen grumbled. "We won't make that mistake again, I can promise you that."

Everyone was quiet for a moment, no one disagreeing with what he had said.

It was Allen who broke the silence. "Sir, it's going to take a hell of a miracle for us to make it out of here alive."

"Um. . ." Lovecraft shuffled nervously on his feet. "I hate to be the one to bring this up but didn't Allen say there was somebody left alive from Wagner's group? Shouldn't we try to locate them before we. . ."

"I said there could be," Allen stopped him. "Not that there was. The number of bodies was one less than what it should have been. That's it. For all we know, those things just dragged it off somewhere to save for later."

"Yeah, Lovecraft! I ain't risking my butt trying to save some guy who is already dead," Dixon growled.

"Corporal!" Callen snapped. "That'll be quite enough."

Dixon bowed his head and shut up, returning his attention to watching the trees beyond the mouth of the cave.

"Allen," Callen said, putting the newbie to the platoon on the spot. "Do you think there could be someone from Wagner's platoon still alive out there?"

"I very much doubt it," Allen frowned. "This whole area is crawling with those beasts. I just don't see how someone could have survived this long. Hell, I almost didn't make it back to you, sir, and I was alone for less than a day."

"You heard the man, Lovecraft," Callen glanced over at the young radio operator and Allen's fellow newbie. "If there was someone who survived the initial attack that wiped those guys out, they have to be dead too by now. There's nothing to keep us here. Our mission is over, we've got the intel we need, and it's time to get the hell out."

"Yes sir," Lovecraft conceded.

"Regardless, we can't go anywhere yet," Allen said. "Those things can see way better in the dark than we can and this is their home too. We go out there right now and we'll be dead before we make it more than a mile or two."

"We wait for the morning," Callen grunted, "but then, we're moving out."

"Should we try to get back into the village?" Dixon asked.

Callen glared at him, knowing what he was thinking. If they went back there and found Lovecraft's radio intact their odds of making it home went up exponentially. To Callen though, it was just far too large of a risk to take. Who knew how long the ape creatures might stick around feeding on the dead or if they were as smart as Allen appeared to apply, the things might even left some of their number to watch the village for more prey to wander into it?

"No," Callen finally answered. "Our best bet is to high tail it back towards Firebase Maria. The sooner we're out of this area, the better."

Lovecraft, having gotten over his moral scruples about leaving without trying to locate the possible survivor from Lieutenant Wagner's platoon, was getting his head back in the game. "Once we cover out of the territory those things consider theirs, we should be fine. They shouldn't have any reason to attack us after that."

Dixon snorted. "Yeah they will, man. Haven't you realized yet that we're food to them? Those things aren't just hunting us because we wandered in here. They're hungry . . .and ticked off too. Bet some of them have got a score to settle with us for taking out their buddies."

"I can't argue with any of that," Lovecraft conceded, "but I still think they'll only follow us so far."

"We move out at dawn," Major Callen grunted. "Dixon, you've got watch. Everyone else, try to get what rest you can."

****

Lieutenant Wagner emerged from the rotting log he'd been hiding in. He'd lost all of track of time. The horrors he'd witnessed had ripped his mind asunder. Wagner muttered to himself as he shoved a worm into his mouth, feeling it wiggle within his cheeks before chewing it up. He'd spent the last few days hiding, running, and waiting for help to come. The monsters were everywhere in the jungle. There was no telling which way they might come at him next. They used the trees they lurked among, traveled through their tops. . .nowhere was safe if you could be seen, heard, or smelt. Only blind luck had kept him alive so far as Wagner saw things. The rifle Wagner dragged along with him contained just four rounds remaining in its magazine. He had no others to reload it with. His pistol was long gone. Wagner had lost it sometime back. He'd lost his knife too along with the rest of his gear. His clothes were in tatters. They'd been torn up by his time in the jungle, catching on the limbs of trees as he ran, picked by the interior of the log he hid in, soaked by blood and rain, covered in mud, and worse. Wagner was a mess in so many ways. . . but he was still alive. He liked to pretend that it mattered, that there was hope.

Nearly letting loose a scream at the top of his lungs and diving back inside the log, Wagner jerked about as he heard a noise amidst the nearby trees. His entire body tensed up, eyes bugging as he feared the monsters had finally found him. He relaxed, breathing a sigh of relief, realizing that the sound had been nothing more than a bird taking flight.

Wagner's stomach rumbled. He leaned back over reaching into the log to extract another worm from its rotting bark. Swallowing it whole, Wagner took another look around making sure the area was really clear of the monsters. He had no idea what the things that killed his men were. The wound on the side of his throat itched badly. Wagner hoped that meant it was healing and not as infected as he figured it was. Tied about his neck was a filthy piece of cloth ripped from the left sleeve of his shirt. It wasn't much of a bandage anymore but he had no replacement for it. The rest of his clothes were just as dirty or more so than it was.

Reaching up to scratch at his makeshift bandage, Wagner grimaced at the pain as his fingers made contact with it. Still, he was thankful. When the beast had grabbed him, Wagner had thought its finger had sunk all the way into his throat and that he would bleed out and die. After escaping the monsters, he discovered it wasn't nearly so bad. Oh, it was bad enough, especially out here, alone, but the thing had merely slashed open a layer of skin, not gone inward as it had seemed to him when it happened.

Stumbling forward, Wagner wandered into the jungle. He didn't really have a plan as to where he was going. Originally, he had been trying to make it back to the firebase his platoon left from but that felt like forever ago. Wagner didn't have a bloody clue which way that was anymore. Something in him told Wagner that he needed to keep moving though. If he stayed anywhere too long, the monsters would find him. That was his thought process anyway.

Wagner looked up at the sky and realized that it was a new day. The sun was just beginning to come up. He sighed, wondering if night and day even had any meaning any longer. To him, they were the same because both were nothing more than a struggle to stay alive. He wandered on through the trees.

Voices up ahead of him froze Wagner in his tracks. The voices were clearly those of men and not the ape creatures. . . and they were speaking English. Wagner was struggling with himself as to whether the voices were real or just inside his mind when a shot rang out. A bullet thudded into a limb of the tree next to him. Splinters exploded outward as the round ruptured its bark. Wagner ducked for cover. He could here men spreading out as if to surround him. More gunshots rang out. Not a single one of them came close to him again. Whoever was shooting didn't appear to know where he was, they only knew that something was out here with them.

Gathering his courage, Wagner shouted, "Hold your fire! I'm American!"

The gunfire stopped instantly.

"Identify yourself!" a gruff voice barked.

"Lieutenant Wagner!" he yelled in response. "Deployed from Firebase Maria. Recon patrol!"

"Holy!" another voice, full of shock and surprise at his answer, cried out.

"Lower your weapon and come out slowly where we can see you, Lieutenant!" a third voice ordered.

Keeping his rifle's barrel aimed at the muddy ground, Wagner walked out of the trees into the small clearing where most of the voices were coming from. He blinked, seeing three soldiers standing there with their weapons pointed at him. Were they real? Wagner honestly didn't know.

"Geez. . .look at him," Wagner heard the youngest of the soldiers say.

"Lieutenant," the soldier who seemed to be in charge barked at him, "I am going to need you to put your weapon on the ground."

"Why?" Wagner snapped back at him.

"I think it would be for the best, Lieutenant," the soldier told him.

"And just who the hell are you to tell me what to do?" Wagner demanded, half tempted to raise his rifle and start shooting.

"I'm Major Callen. My men and I were dispatched from Firebase Maria just like your platoon was. We were sent to find you and bring you home."

Lieutenant Wagner was trembling. The major's words jarred him to his core. Could help really finally have come? Did he trust his mind, these people, enough to put down his weapon? Was it worth the risk?

Before Wagner could decide what to do, another soldier jumped him from behind. The guy was fast as hell. He snatched Wagner's rifle from his grasp and threw it towards the soldiers. Wagner tried to fight back, taking a swing at him. The soldier deftly blocked the blow and delivered a kick to Wagner's stomach that sent him toppling over into the mud.

"I suggest you stay down, sir," the soldier said, towering over him. "I don't want to have to hurt you."

Snarling like one of the beasts he'd spent so long running and hiding from, Wagner leaped up at the soldier. The butt of a rifle met his forehead with a loud thunk as Wagner's world went dark.

****

"Allen!" Major Callen shouted, hoping the man hadn't killed the man they were after.

"Don't worry, sir," Allen said, "I didn't hit him that hard."

Lovecraft rushed over to where Lieutenant Wagner lay, sprawled out, and squatted so that he could check him out.

"He's just out cold, sir," Lovecraft reported. "The lieutenant should be fine when he wakes up."

"Gonna have one hell of a headache though," Dixon chuckled and then walked over closer to Allen. "Remind me never to tick you off."

"Lieutenant or not, this guy has clearly lost it," Allen shrugged. "Didn't you see the look in his eyes? I've seen that kind of look before. It's a wonder he didn't come out of the trees shooting at us."

"Frag it," Major Callen grumbled. "We're going to have to take him with us. We can't leave him out here. Lovecraft, do what you can for his wounds and then tie up his hands. Dixon, you think you can carry the lieutenant until he comes around?"

Dixon glared at Callen. "You're kidding me, right?"

Major Callen glared right back at him.

"Oh, fragging Hell," Dixon relented. "I can carry him but y'all better be ready to cover me if those ape things find us."

Major Callen walked over to where Lovecraft was beginning to tend to Wagner. "How bad is he hurt?"

"You can see he's got a nasty wound on his neck, sir. It's infected," Lovecraft frowned. "Nothing else that appears to be serious. Just exhaustion and dehydration otherwise."

A few minutes later, the group was on the move again. Dixon had Wagner hefted up over his shoulder with the lieutenant's head dangling down behind his back. The sky above was clear and blue. The rains of the night before had ended with the dawn. The heat in the jungle was already nearly unbearable. Major Callen ran the back of his hand across his forehead to wipe away the sweat there before it could drip down into his eyes.

He didn't envy Dixon's job of carrying Wagner. The going was slow as they all trudged through the jungle. On the upside, there hadn't been any sign of the ape creatures yet. No one knew exactly how much ground they needed to cover to get beyond the point where the things would follow them but Major Callen figured that they had a long way to go.

As the day wore on, the heat only got worse. Lieutenant Wagner had regained consciousness. He was walking on his own now. The man really wasn't right in the head. Wagner had never been much of an officer from what Callen had heard. The guy was a career paper pusher who had just wanted to see some real action before the war was over and he was shipped back home. Pulling some strings and calling favors, Wagner ended up out here and surely, he had enough of his mind left to do so, regretted it. Callen saw Wagner as not much more than an unneeded danger to them at this point but he had a duty to get the man home.

"Hold up," Major Callen ordered. Everyone was on the verge of collapse. They had stumbled upon a small clearing and it was as good a place as any to get some rest. Getting their bearings again would be a good thing to do as well. "Everybody take ten."

Callen saw Allen give him a look of disapproval. The killer wanted the hell out of the jungle ASAP. Callen couldn't blame him. He'd been forced to survive on his own out here unlike any of the rest of them other than Wagner . . . and Wagner had been broken by it.

"Gotta rest some or we'll never make it," Callen said to Allen, attempting to justify his call for a break even though he didn't need to.

Dixon all but collapsed as soon as Callen ordered the break. He sat slumped against the trunk of a tree, his rifle resting in his lap. Lovecraft was trying to keep Wagner under control. The lieutenant was freaking out and babbling about the monsters that were coming to get them.

Allen walked over to Callen, keeping his voice low. "I hate to say it, sir, but that whacko is right. Those things are out there and eventually, they will find us. There's no way we're going to be able to cover enough ground fast enough for them not to."

Callen nodded. He agreed with the killer's assessment but there wasn't a blasted thing he could do about it except keep pushing on and hoping for the best. Digging his pack of cigarettes out of his pocket, Callen lit up. It was his last one. He crumpled the empty pack and let it drop into the grass and mud. That was when he saw the creature. On the far side of the clearing, an ape creature was perched in the branches of a tall tree, watching them with its glowing, yellow eyes. The thing was completely motionless, sitting there like a statue carved from stone. Callen was afraid to move or try to warn Allen of the creature's presence. He didn't want to set it off because where there was one, there was likely a lot more. Thankfully, he realized, Allen had seen the ape creature too. The killer nodded subtly in its direction. Callen nodded back, letting Allen know that he was aware of it.

At that moment, Lieutenant Wagner totally flipped out without warning. He took off, running across the clearing, howling at the top of his lungs.

"Stop!" Callen shouted, trying to grab Wagner as the lieutenant passed by him. His fingers caught part of Wagner's uniform but the already tattered cloth merely ripped away from him.

The bait that Wagner unintentionally gave the monster in the tree was too tempting for the thing to resist. Surrendering its hiding place among the limbs and thick leaves, the ape creature sprang out at Wagner. The lieutenant's wild cries rose to shrieks of absolute terror as the beast slammed into him. Its weight knocked Wagner to the ground beneath it. Wagner thrashed about trying to get the ape creature off of him. The beast snatched up a rock that was the size of a man's hand and brought it down onto the lieutenant's nose with the sharp, loud sound of breaking bone. Its next blow cracked his right eye socket. The ape creature raised the rock again and Wagner's forehead folded inward as the rock struck him. The thrashing of his body intensified though it was different now. The movements had become the lieutenant's death throes.

Allen was carrying several weapons but it was a pump action combat shotgun that was in his hands at the moment. Working its pump, the killer chambered a round, rushing forward. The shotgun thundered as Allen blew the ape creature's head into a mess of exploding pulp and bone fragments. The ape creature flopped over backwards, falling away from where it sat atop Wagner's corpse.

"More are coming!" Allen yelled in warning.

Callen and the others heard the monsters coming before they saw them. Three more of the ape creatures were leaping from tree top to tree top, closing in fast, each from a different direction.

There was no sign of the creatures on the ground, only the ones in the trees. For some reason he couldn't explain, that worried Callen. Regardless, soon enough, there would be more of the beasts. Every one of the monsters within earshot of the clearing would surely hear the sounds of the battle and be drawn to it.

The three ape creatures leaped from the trees onto the ground. Two of them rushed Allen, the other went after Lovecraft. Seeing Dixon moving to help the young radio operator, Callen took aim at those going after Allen. His M14 cracked in rapid succession as Callen let loose, trying to stop at least one of the monsters. The beast wailed as his bullets ripped and tore at the hair-covered flesh of its back. It stumbled, falling onto its hands and knees. The ape creature's head swung around, its yellow eyes burning with rage. Heaving itself to his feet, the beast, forgetting about Allen, charged him as Callen opened up on it again. A bullet clipped the beast's left shoulder while another tore into the flesh of its arm. The creature's too human face was twisted into a snarl. The next thing Callen knew, the creature had closed the distance between them and was wrenching his rifle from his hands. Callen recoiled from the monster as it threw his rifle away into the trees. His hand went for the pistol holstered on his hip but before he could reach it, the monster took a swing at him, its claws slashing through the air at his face. Callen avoided the blow, narrowly, losing his balance in the process. He fell to the ground, staring up at the beast as it towered over him. In disbelief, Callen watched as Allen, seemingly coming out of nowhere, jumped onto the monster's back. The killer's right hand dragged the blade of a large knife across its throat. Blood splattered in an explosion of red. The beast reeled away, clutching at its neck. Allen had flung himself away from it, landing deftly on his feet, with almost inhuman agility. His expression was that of a feral cat pleased with the torture it had inflicted upon its prey.

"Get up!" Allen barked at him though Major Callen was already scrambling back onto his feet.

Allen shrugged a rifle from where it hung over his back by its strap, tossing the weapon to Callen, who deftly snatched the weapon from the air.

"Thanks." Callen gave him a quick nod.

Lovecraft ran for his fragging life. His legs pumping beneath him, he sucked gulps of air into his lungs. Skin gone pale and eyes bugging,

Lovecraft had never been so terrified. He could hear the heavy thuds of the ape creature's footfalls drawing closer behind him. Lovecraft didn't dare risk a glance over his shoulder to see how close the monster was but he knew it was gaining on him with each step. The young radio operator figured there were only a few moments remaining in his life before the beast was within reach and the fingers of its hands closed upon him.

Dixon sprinted after the ape creature chasing Lovecraft, cursing the kid for running instead of standing his ground. He couldn't risk a shot at the monster without taking a chance of hitting Lovecraft. . .at least until the two of them stopped. Of course, if he waited for them to do that, Lovecraft would likely be dead. The ape creature would tear into the kid before anything he could do would matter. Pushing himself on even faster, Dixon came up with an insane plan. He took aim carefully and fired, not at the beast, but at a tree next to it as the thing kept running. His rounds found their target. The bark exploded sending splinters flying. Several of them struck the beast. The thing whirled around, its yellow eyes blazing with primal rage. Dixon couldn't help but flash a wry grin and the ape creature bounded towards him.

The sound of his shots and the minor wounds they inflicted as they hit the tree had done the trick in getting its attention.

The beast came at him like a freight train, fast and muscles bulging. The claws on his hands gleamed in the light of the midday sun. Its jagged teeth were bared, black lips parted. Dixon fired two careful shots, each blowing apart one of the ape creature's eyes inside their sockets. Blinded and in what must have been near unbearable pain, the beast changed its course, bounding away. It ran straight into the trunk of a tree. The beast hit with such force that the tree was nearly uprooted, cracks snaking across its trunk. Its bones broke inside of the creature too from the impact and its limp body bounced backwards to land sprawled out upon the ground.

"Lovecraft!" Dixon yelled, trying to get the young radio operator's attention but the kid was still sprinting away. Dixon spat, "Frag!"

The kid could run. Dixon gave him that but not much else.

"Lovecraft! Damn it, kid! You can stop running now!" Dixon called after him.

This time, his words must have gotten through to the kid because Lovecraft skidded to a halt.

Dixon was moving so fast he almost ran into him. Lovecraft fell onto him, arms hugging around Dixon who roughly shoved the kid away.

"Get yourself together," Dixon ordered Lovecraft. "We've got to get back. The others need our help."

Lovecraft's head bobbed furiously.

They rushed back towards the clearing. Ahead of them there was no sounds of gunfire or the monsters either. As the two of them emerged from the jungle, Dixon saw the other ape creatures lying dead. Allen and the major were both still standing.

"Dixon, Lovecraft," Major Callen said. "Glad to see you're still alive."

"Sir," Allen snapped.

"I know," Callen nodded. "Come on. There will be more of those things here any second and we don't want to still be around when they show up."

****

The whole jungle seemed to be alive with the grunts, snarls, and bestial cries of the ape creatures. They rang out from every direction. Allen was in the lead as the group moved as fast as they could through the trees. Callen watched the killer ahead of him and was impressed by both his agility and endurance.

Then suddenly the jungle opened up onto the bank of a wide river. Allen didn't slow at all but rather plunged right into its water. He was swimming across it like a mad devil fleeing the fires of hell. Callen paused, letting Lovecraft and Dixon go on ahead of him. They followed Allen's example.

Callen remained on the river's bank long enough to get a good look back at the jungle they were leaving behind. He counted more than a dozen of the ape creatures in the trees and amid them. Reaching into his pocket, his fingers closed on the Willie Pete grenade Allen had given him after their escape from the village. Callen popped its pin.

"Come and get this, you fragger!" Callen bellowed, throwing the grenade at the largest cluster of the approaching ape creatures. The grenade detonated in a flash of white hot flames setting several of the beasts and the trees around them on fire. The flames spread outward as they continued to burn and a cloud of white smoke grew, blocking Callen's view. He could hear the shrieks and wails of the monsters, hoping they all were being returned to whatever hell they had climbed out of.

Callen dived into the water. Arms and legs kicking, he swam on after the others. Allen was already exiting the river on its opposite side, dripping as he climbed up it, weapons still swinging by their straps upon his back. Dixon emerged from the water next to help Allen drag Lovecraft out of it. As soon as the young radio operator lay on the riverbank, gasping and shivering despite the heat, Allen's head was up, looking around.

Reaching the shore near them, with a grunt of effort, Major Callen heaved himself up onto it. Callen was amazed that he had managed to keep his hold on his rifle. He was likely going to need it yet.

"Did it work?" Lovecraft blurted out. "Are we safe now?"

"What?" Callen asked.

"Crossing the water?" Lovecraft said. "Will it keep them away? I read somewhere that big ape creatures like that can't swim."

"I figured it was the Willie Pete you hit them with over there that was keeping them back,"

Dixon huffed. "But maybe Lovecraft's onto something. Ain't none of those things trying to swim over here. That's for sure but dang. . . you can still hear them howling."

Howling wasn't the word Callen would have used to describe the cries of the distant ape creatures. There was still some louder, pain filled cries but beyond the thick cloud of white smoke which obscured the river bank across from them there were also grunts of rage that were just as loud. Regardless of what was keeping the apes from entering the water, something surely was.

"Ain't nothing stopping them from crossing that though," Allen pointed to the south.

Callen had to squint against the sun to see it but when he did, his hope that they had finally truly escaped the ape creatures died within him. About half a mile down river was a bridge.

"Won't take those things long to find it," Allen gritted his teeth. "Assuming they don't already know it's there."

"Fragging hell," Callen snarled.

"Let's not just hang around here waiting on them then," Dixon urged.

"I got point," Dixon announced, darting ahead before either Callen or Allen could stop him.

Allen looked at Callen and shrugged. What choice did they have but to follow Dixon?

Dixon set a fast pace for the rest of them, too fast for Callen's liking. Lovecraft was having a devil of a time trying to keep up. The kid was huffing and puffing so hard that Callen wondered if he was about to pass out. They'd all been through hell and the kid was a newbie after all. Callen couldn't do anything to help him. It was up to the kid to find the strength to keep going. If Lovecraft failed to muster it up, well, he'd deal with that when it happened.

They had been on the move for close to ten minutes by Callen's best estimate when they burst out of the jungle onto a dirt road.

"Frag yeah!" Dixon yelled, thrusting his rifle up into the air sideways above his head.

Callen understood why. He recognized the road too. The copter that brought them in had flown over it. Reaching the road meant not only that they were on the right track back to Firebase Maria but with any luck that had finally escaped the portion of the jungle belonging to the ape creatures. It was unlikely that the things would enter such a well-traveled portion of the world ruled by men.

He saw Lovecraft looking at him with hopeful eyes, waiting on Callen to confirm Dixon's shouts of triumph as Allen stood peering into the tress behind them. Callen wasn't ready to relax just yet. There was no certainty that the ape creatures wouldn't come after them even if it meant venturing into the world of man given the deaths they had dealt out upon the things.

No one could have seen what was coming at them next but rightfully, all of them should have. The grenade came flying from the trees on the far side of the road, landing near Dixon, where he continued to dance about in gleeful victory. Its blast was thunderous. Dixon never knew what hit him. The shrapnel shredded his legs and abdomen, impaling itself in his face and neck. His death was nigh instantaneous aside from a fleeting moment of pain. Callen had caught a glimpse of the grenade before it hit the ground and threw himself off the side of the road. Allen also managed to avoid the fury of its blast, jumping into the trees. Poor Lovecraft though, the kid wasn't so lucky.

Lovecraft screamed as a piece of shrapnel from the grenade imbedded itself in his upper thigh and he was blown from his feet. He was flung onto the dirt of the road, rolling. The impact knocked

Lovecraft's breath from his lungs in a pained grunt that emptied them entirely.

AK-47s chattered in the wake of the blast. Rounds fired from them threw up puffs of dirt and dust along the road, working their way towards Major Callen as the Viet Cong attempted to end him where he was. Hurling himself to his feet, Callen dived into the cover of the trees. He heard Allen's shotgun answering the incoming fire in kind. It thundered and then thundered again. Callen pulled himself up behind the trunk of a tree, leaning around it. He couldn't see the Viet Cong on the other side of the road but opened up at where their fire was coming from. Someone amid the trees there cried out.

It was impossible to know for sure how many of the Viet Cong they were up against. It could be a handful on patrol or an entire platoon. Either way, Callen hadn't come this far to be killed by them in a fragging ambush.

"Major!" Lovecraft squealed from where he crawled across the road, leaving a trail of red in his wake. Blood was pouring from the wound in his thigh. "Help me!"

Callen scowling, put another burst of rounds in the trees where the Viet Cong had to be. He had watched so many of his men die in the last forty-eight hours.

"Cover me!" Callen yelled at Allen then darted out from behind the tree he was using as cover onto the road. He sprinted towards Lovecraft. Callen was halfway to him when something stung his left shoulder so badly that he lost his hold on his rifle. It fell onto the road as he kept running. Callen reached Lovecraft, leaning over to yank the kid up. Lovecraft's arm was flung over his neck as Callen half carried, half dragged the young radio operator back the way he'd come. A bullet whizzed by his head.

Allen's shotgun boomed in rapid succession as fast as the killer could pump rounds into its chamber. When it clicked empty, he tossed it aside, swinging an M14 from where it hung on his back into his hands. Allen's finger worked its trigger, continuing to put as many rounds as he could into the trees across the road from him.

Callen and Lovecraft made it to the cover of the trees. Lovecraft thudded onto the ground as Callen let him go, slumping behind a tree as bullets bit into its bark on its other side.

"For frag's sake, kid!" Callen shouted. "Get your leg tied off or you'll bleed out."

Lovecraft appeared to understand him. The young radio operator tore at the sleeve of his uniform weakly, trying to do what Callen had ordered him.

Callen could see Allen close by, still trying to keep the Viet Cong at bay. Allen was like a one man army as he popped another series of shots and another voice screamed from the tree across the road.

Then suddenly, there was a lot of screams from those trees. Numerous voices crying out in terrified surprise and utter fear. Callen noticed there were no more shots coming their way but the gunfire of the Viet Cong sounded more frantic than it had. What the Hell? He wondered for a split second then somehow, he knew. He just knew what was happening, putting two and two together.

Allen's fire had also fallen silent. The killer came running over.

"It's them," Allen warned. "Has to be."

Callen nodded.

Lovecraft had managed to tie a makeshift tourniquet about his wounded thigh. There was still blood seeping through it but the effort had stemmed its flow some, enough to keep the young radio operator alive and conscious, for the time being at any rate.

The gunfire and screams fell silent. Callen and the killer exchanged a look.

"I've only got one magazine left," Allen said grimly.

"You still got that last WP grenade?" Callen asked.

Allen nodded.

"Keep it ready," Callen ordered. "We're going to need it."

Lovecraft was whimpering despite his best efforts to fight off the pain he was in and keep himself together.

The headless corpse of a Viet Cong soldier was flung from the trees facing them. The corpse landed so hard on the road that it bounced several times before finally coming to a stop.

"Oh fragging hell," Allen muttered.

The beast sauntered out onto the road. It was the largest of the ape creatures they had seen. The monster stood a towering eight feet tall, all thick muscle and burning rage. The hair covering its body was brownish red that matched the blazing of its eyes. This one's eyes were blood red. There was no doubt that it was the alpha male, the leader of the creatures that had followed them here.

"God help us," Callen breathed.

"What. . .what the hell does it want?" Lovecraft mumbled, tears running down his cheeks.

"Vengeance," Allen said in a cold, hard voice that left no room for argument. "It wants blood for blood. We killed its brothers and sisters and there has to be retribution."

Callen cut his eyes at the killer. It really was that simple, wasn't it?

The beast stood upon the road, breathing hard, watching them with its hands curled into fists hanging by its sides.

"I'd wager that thing came alone," Allen said. "At least we got that going for us."

Callen realized that he was weaponless. The cloth of his shirt was soaked red with blood that leaked from the bullet hole in his shoulder. The round had gone through cleanly and the adrenaline coursing through him had prevented Callen from feeling the pain until now. He clapped a hand over the wound, bracing himself.

As if reading his mind, Allen drew closer, extending the butt of a pistol to him.

"Take it, Major," Allen ordered.

Callen accepted the weapon, frowning. "And

if we kill this one, is it really over?"

"War is never over," Allen grunted. "Not for men like us."

The ape creature continued to stare at them. Callen felt its red eyes burning into the depths of his soul.

"Well, I, for one, aim to finish this," Callen said. "Let's get this the hell over with."

"Help me up," Lovecraft shouted at Allen. "I'm not just going to lay here waiting to die."

Allen got the young radio operator onto his feet. Lovecraft found his balance, though painfully. Allen saw that Lovecraft couldn't hold a rifle and support himself so he produced another small pistol that had been strapped to his boot. He pressed it into Lovecraft's right hand.

"Hang on to that, kid," Allen told him.

The beast was getting tired of waiting on them to come out and face it. Leaning forward, the creature roared, pounding at its chest.

The three soldiers walked out onto the road, standing in front of the beast, several yards away from it. The scene reminded Callen of something akin to gunfighters in an old Western. It was Allen who made the first move. The barrel of his M14 came up, blazing, as Allen stroked the rifle's trigger, firing a series of shots at the hulking beast. The ape creature dove to the right, avoiding the bulk of the killer's shots. The few that hit the beast appeared to do little more than further anger the thing.

Callen's pistol barked as he fired a shot that clipped the side of the monster's right arm, drawing blood there beneath the hair covering it. With a trembling hand, Lovecraft got off a shot too. It went wide of the beast.

The alpha ape moved with such speed it closed the distance between itself and the trio of soldiers in the span of a heartbeat. One of its large fists slammed into Allen with such force that he was lifted from the road and flung back into the trees at its side. Then the monster turned its attention to Lovecraft, who was stumbling towards it, firing his pistol over and over. Each shot hammered into the alpha ape's chest. Blood splattered at they buried themselves in its flesh. The hulking monster roared, springing at the young radio operator. Lovecraft didn't have a chance in hell of dodging its attack as he was barely staying on his feet as it was. The ape creature grabbed Lovecraft by the sides of his face and popped his head like an overripe melon. Gore splashed into the air, covering the beast in its red wetness.

Callen stood alone against the monster now. Lovecraft was dead and Allen had yet to emerge from the trees. He didn't even know if the killer was still alive and couldn't count on his help. Callen's pistol was aimed the hulking monster as it moved slowly towards him, as if he was nothing to it. He allowed the thing to approach him though it took all his nerve. There was only one way to end things, Callen realized.

The beast lunged forward, grabbing him up into its arms. Callen made no effort to dodge but did twist about so that his own arms were free within its grip. As the monster hugged him to its chest, crushing him, Callen felt the bones of his ribcage collapsing. The taste of his blood filled his mouth as it rose up his throat. He couldn't breathe and never would again. The beast had done its damage. . .but he would do his as well. Pressing the barrel of his pistol to the side of the ape creature's head, Callen got his vengeance. He emptied the weapon into the monster. The bullets blew the monster's brain apart inside of its skull. Its grip on him loosened. Callen slid free of its arms as both he and the monster toppled onto the road. The monster's corpse lay twitching and bucking about until it finally lay still. Callen's own body was sprawled out beside it. Blood leaked from the corners of his mouth as he struggled to take a breath and failed. Pain was all he knew until at last his world blessedly went dark.

****

Allen came awake screaming. Hands grappled him, forcing his body back down onto the bed it rose from.

"Stop it, man!" a stern voice shouted at him. "You're safe now!"

Shaking his head wildly, Allen began to return to his senses. He looked around and saw that he was in a medical tent.

"Where am I?" Allen croaked.

"Firebase Maria," the medic who had kept him from getting up told him. "From what I hear you're fragging lucky to be here too. Those Viet Cong bastards really did a number on the guys they found you with."

"Major Callen, is he. . .?" Allen started.

"Dead," the medic frowned. "They all are. You were the only one from your entire platoon that made it back."

The medic patted him on the arm. "Get some

rest. I'll be back to check on you later."

Allen watched the medic walk on to attend to his next patient and then closed his eyes, sliding once again into the world of sleep. . . and nightmares. The apes were waiting for him.

The End

Eric S. Brown is the author of numerous book series including the Bigfoot War series, the Psi-Mechs Inc. series, the Kaiju Apocalypse series (with Jason Cordova), the Crypto-Squad series (with Jason Brannon), the Homeworld series (With Tony Faville and Jason Cordova), the Jack Bunny Bam series, and the A Pack of Wolves series. Some of his stand-alone books include War of the Worlds plus Blood Guts and Zombies, Casper Alamo (with Jason Brannon), Sasquatch Island, Day of the Sasquatch, Bigfoot, Crashed, World War of the Dead, Last Stand in a Dead Land, Sasquatch Lake, Kaiju Armageddon, Megalodon, Megalodon Apocalypse, Kraken, Alien Battalion, The Last Fleet, and From the Snow They Came to name only a few. His short fiction has been published hundreds of times in the small press in beyond including markets like the Onward Drake and Black Tide Rising anthologies from Baen Books, the Grantville Gazette, the SNAFU Military horror anthology series, and Walmart World magazine. He has done the novelizations for such films as Boggy Creek: The Legend is True (Studio 3 Entertainment) and The Bloody Rage of Bigfoot (Great Lake films). The first book of his Bigfoot War series was adapted into a feature film by Origin Releasing in 2014. Werewolf Massacre at Hell's Gate was the second of his books to be adapted into film in 2015. Major Japanese publisher, Takeshobo, bought the reprint rights to his Kaiju Apocalypse series (with Jason Cordova) and the mass market, Japanese language version was released in late 2017. Ring of Fire Press has released a collected edition of his Monster Society stories (set in the New York Times Best-selling world of Eric Flint's 1632). In addition to his fiction, Eric also writes an award-winning comic book news column entitled "Comics in a Flash" as well a pop culture column for Altered Reality Magazine. Eric lives in North Carolina with his wife and two children where he continues to write tales of the hungry dead, blazing guns, and the things that lurk in the woods.

Check out other great

Cryptid Novels!

J.H. Moncrieff

RETURN TO DYATLOV PASS

In 1959, nine Russian students set off on a skiing expedition in the Ural Mountains. Their mutilated bodies were discovered weeks later. Their bizarre and unexplained deaths are one of the most enduring true mysteries of our time. Nearly sixty years later, podcast host Nat McPherson ventures into the same mountains with her team, determined to finally solve the mystery of the Dyatlov Pass incident. Her plans are thwarted on the first night, when two trackers from her group are brutally slaughtered. The team's guide, a superstitious man from a neighboring village, blames the killings on yetis, but no one believes him. As members of Nat's team die one by one, she must figure out if there's a murderer in their midst—or something even worse—before history repeats itself and her group becomes another casualty of the infamous Dead Mountain.

Gerry Griffiths

CRYPTID ZOO

As a child, rare and unusual animals, especially cryptid creatures, always fascinated Carter Wilde. Now that he's an eccentric billionaire and runs the largest conglomerate of high-tech companies all over the world, he can finally achieve his wildest dream of building the most incredible theme park ever conceived on the planet... CRYPTID ZOO. Even though there have been apparent problems with the project, Wilde still decides to send some of his marketing employees and their families on a forced vacation to assess the theme park in preparation for Opening Day. Nick Wells and his family are some of those chosen and are about to embark on what will become the most terror-filled weekend of their lives—praying they survive. STEP RIGHT UP AND GET YOUR FREE PASS... TO CRYPTID ZOO

Check out other great

Cryptid Novels!

Hunter Shea

LOCH NESS REVENGE

Deep in the murky waters of Loch Ness, the creature known as Nessie has returned. Twins Natalie and Austin McQueen watched in horror as their parents were devoured by the world's most infamous lake monster. Two decades later, it's their turn to hunt the legend. But what lurks in the Loch is not what they expected. Nessie is devouring everything in and around the Loch, and it's not alone. Hell has come to the Scottish Highlands. In a fierce battle between man and monster, the world may never be the same. Praise for THEY RISE : "Outrageous, balls to the wall...made me yearn for 3D glasses and a tub of popcorn, extra butter!" – The Eyes of Madness "A fast-paced, gore-heavy splatter fest of sharksploitation." The Werd "A rocket paced horror story. I enjoyed the hell out of this book." Shotgun Logic Reviews

C.G. Mosley

BAKER COUNTY BIGFOOT CHRONICLE

Marie Bledsoe only wants her missing brother Kurt back. She'll stop at nothing to make it happen and, with the help of Kurt's friend Tony, along with Sheriff Ray Cochran, Marie embarks on a terrifying journey deep into the belly of the mysterious Walker Laboratory to find him. However, what she and her companions find lurking in the laboratory basement is beyond comprehension. There are cryptids from the forest being held captive there and something...else. Enjoy this suspenseful tale from the mind of C.G. Mosley, author of Wood Ape. Welcome back to Baker County, a place where monsters do lurk in the night!

@severedpress
/severedpress

Check out other great

Cryptid Novels!

P.K. Hawkins

THE CRYPTID FILES

Fresh out of the academy with top marks, Agent Bradley Tennyson is expecting to have the pick of cases and investigations throughout the country. So he's shocked when instead he is assigned as the new partner to "The Crag," an agent well past his prime. He thinks the assignment is a punishment. It's anything but.Agent George Crag has been doing this job for far longer than most, and he knows what skeletons his bosses have in the closet and where the bodies are buried. He has pretty much free reign to pick his cases, and he knows exactly which one he wants to use to break in his new young partner: the disappearance and murder of a couple of college kids in a remote mountain town.Tennyson doesn't realize it, but Crag is about to introduce him to a world he never believed existed: The Cryptid Files, a world of strange monsters roaming in the night. Because these murders have been going on for a long time, and evidence is mounting that the murderer may just in fact be the legendary Bigfoot.

Gerry Griffiths

DOWN FROM BEAST MOUNTAIN

A beast with a grudge has come down from the mountain to terrorize the townsfolk of Porterville. The once sleepy town is suddenly wide awake. Sheriff Abel McGuire and game warden Grant Tanner frantically investigate one brutal slaying after another as they follow the blood trail they hope will eventually lead to the monstrous killer. But they better hurry and stop the carnage before the census taker has to come out and change the population sign on the edge of town to ZERO.

Printed in Great Britain
by Amazon